Last Chance Lake

Last Chance Ranch Book 5

Liz Isaacson

ISBN-13: 978-1638761495

Chapter One

Cache Bryant sat on the front steps of his cabin, his acoustic guitar across his lap as he watched the sun rise in front of him. The golden rays filled his soul with light and peace, and he loved this time of the morning.

Before dawn, he didn't have to worry about his tasks for today. He didn't worry about the bills he had to pay, or the cows he had to train, or the woman he wanted to impress.

Cache enjoyed the moment while he could, because he had a lot to do today. Scarlett, the owner of Last Chance Ranch, had been hounding him about getting the cow cuddling up and running. She simply had no idea how much work it took to make a bovine lay down and be petted. It wasn't natural for cows, though Cache had found that they liked it.

But cows were stubborn, and the training had taken

longer than he'd anticipated. Than anyone had anticipated.

As they were wont to do, his thoughts wandered first to his family's dairy farm in Nevada. They'd lost it a couple of years ago, and Cache had come further west to Last Chance Ranch while his brother and father had gone east to Shiloh Ridge in the panhandle of Texas.

Maybe he just needed to go visit them. Get a change of scenery for a few days. He wasn't sure, but the funk he'd fallen into recently seemed to be plaguing him for longer than usual.

He liked his job here at Last Chance Ranch. He did. He loved the people, though he was feeling particularly lonely now that Sawyer was married and Dave had started dating Sissy. Cache felt like so much of his life had passed him by, while he watched the sun rise and dreamed of milking cows.

But it was his life, and he actually enjoyed it—most of the time.

He sighed as he got to his feet. After taking his guitar inside and propping it in the corner against the coat closet, he grabbed his work gloves from the end table near the couch and headed out.

"Mornin'," Dave said as he moved down his front steps too, and Cache smiled at him.

"Yep, it's morning again," Cache said. They started down the road together, though Dave sometimes drove his truck over to the stables where he worked. Cache had worked jobs all over the ranch, but he'd traded out his time on the south side of the ranch with the bigger animals to administer meds to the horses for the large care vet. And when he wasn't doing that, he worked in the Canine Club or with his dairy cows.

Last Chance Ranch wasn't really set up to be a dairy operation, and his cows' milk had dried up a while ago. They grazed, and lowed at the chickens that got out of their coops, and hopefully, Cache could start getting people into the pasture for the cuddling.

"How are the cows doing?" Dave asked, and it seemed that was all anyone asked Cache.

"Great," he said. "How's the new dog?"

A smile spread across Dave's face. "Awesome. I might get another one."

"They're all over anyway," Cache said, smiling. A couple of cars turned onto the road behind them, and Cache moved to the side. "Goat yoga this morning."

"I don't understand it," Dave said.

"Yeah." Cache said nothing about the cuddling. Until they were ready to launch the program, Scarlett had sworn him to secrecy. She wouldn't even tell Karla, the ranch's marketing director, and surely she'd need time to put together something for the announcement of the program.

Cache wasn't sure. What he knew was limited, only what he could glean from a couple of articles online about a farm in New England. Connecticut, if he remembered right. If there were other farms or ranches picking up on the idea, he hadn't heard of them.

"Band practice Friday?" Dave asked.

"Yeah," Cache said, wishing he had a date on Friday night. He could ask someone, he knew. Plenty of women came to the ranch each day, from volunteers to regular employees like the new veterinarian technician Scarlett had hired a few months ago.

"Got any new songs?" Dave asked, and Cache finally started to feel more like himself.

"Yeah," he said. "And Sawyer's said he'll have one too. Apparently, being awake in the middle of the night with a baby has helped his creativity."

Dave chuckled with Cache. "Yeah, I bet."

"Cute baby they brought home," Cache said.

"Totally," Dave said, keeping his gaze down the road as they passed in front of the homestead.

"I'll see you later," Cache said, detouring to the right while Dave kept going. The administration building was down that way, and Dave had taken to stopping by that building in the morning since he'd started seeing Sissy more often.

Cache hadn't asked him specifically about her, but Dave had been in an increasingly good mood the past month or so, and Sissy had been the only thing in his life that had changed. Cache could put two and two together.

He cleaned out the watering troughs for the llamas and refilled them, enjoying the crisp start to the day. He took a deep breath and got to work measuring the medicines Blade needed that day.

Everything about a living, breathing, working ranch enthralled him, and always had. He loved the circle of life, even when sometimes he lost a horse or a cow or a dog.

After getting all the medicines to all the right equines, he headed back toward the homestead, where the twelve dairy cows he'd been training were housed in a huge field across the dirt lane from the cabins that bordered the backyard of the homestead. The rest of the bovines were kept in a different field between the homestead and the Goat Grounds.

He couldn't help glancing to the row of cabins there. Gramps lived in the end one, and Cache loved the old man as if he were his own grandfather. Adele and Carson lived in the one in the middle, and Karla Jenkins lived in the third.

Karla Jenkins.

The woman Cache had been trying to impress for a while now. He'd invited her to the Halloween carnival eight months ago so she could see his band. She'd come, and she'd clapped and laughed along with everyone else.

But she hadn't gushed over him the way the girls did to Dave. Cache could sing too, but his first love was the guitar. His second was these insufferable cows, and he jumped over the fence to join them in the pasture.

He whistled at them as if they were dogs, and several turned toward him. "Cookie. Daisy. Come on, girls."

Some of the cows he'd named and could tell them one from another. Only about eight or nine of them, the ones he'd been working with tirelessly to get them to lay down on command.

His cows lumbered toward him, all but two who stayed stubbornly out in the field a ways, already lying down. He didn't whistle again, as he'd been working for months to get Jenny and Flower to lie down and stay there.

He went to them instead, starting to talk to them the closer he got. "What's going on with you two?" he asked. "Are you sick?"

His other cuddlers came with him, their footsteps heavy in the grass. He avoided a spot of cow manure, asking, "Flower, what are you doing?" He reached the cow and ran his hand down her side. She didn't seem to be bloated.

"What—?" It was then that he saw the sandy blonde hair of a woman curled into the cow's chest.

Karla Jenkins herself tilted her head back and looked up at him. A smile sprang to her face, and she looked like a bright ray of heaven. "Morning."

"Good morning," he said, glad it was a natural reaction and he didn't have to think to do it. Karla Jenkins, out in his cow pasture, cuddling his cows. He had no idea what to make of it.

"What are you doing here?" he asked, staring openly at her. She'd been in his dreams for months, and yet she'd never really indicated that she was interested in him at all.

"Scarlett told me you were training your cows for a cuddling thing," she said. "I thought I'd try it. Is this how it's done?"

Cache wanted to blurt that her cuddling into Flower's side was one of the sexiest things he'd ever seen. Instead, he just nodded. "They've only had me to practice with," he said.

"I'm happy to volunteer as a test subject," she said.

"You could get kicked."

She smiled at him again. "Oh, I don't think so. This cow is nothing but a sweetheart." She patted Flower's ribcage.

Cache chuckled, some of the awkwardness between him and Karla leaking away. It didn't seem fair, though, that she had to be here, looking so soft and lovely and cuddling with his cow.

Maybe he could just ask her to dinner. He'd never really come out and asked. Maybe he was absolutely terrible at flirting and needed to be more forthright.

"Cache," she said, and he blinked himself back into focusing on her.

"Yeah?"

She stood up and brushed dirt and grass from her clothes. She wore a pair of khaki shorts and a cute T-shirt with lemons on it. "I didn't mean to step on your toes."

"You didn't," he said. "I was just surprised. Scarlett didn't want anyone to know about the cow cuddling."

Karla ran her fingers through her hair, driving Cache toward the brink of madness.

"You wouldn't want to...I don't know. Go to dinner with me. Would you?" Cache swallowed, and he swore Flower sighed as if to say, *Oh, buddy, bad idea.*

Karla blinked, shock traveling across her face in slow waves. "Dinner?"

"Yeah, dinner," Cache said boldly, refusing to look away. No more games. No more dancing around this woman at the meals she cooked for the whole ranch.

The longer she stood there and stared at him, framed by his lounging cows, the stupider Cache felt. Was she going to say anything? He'd even take a no at this point. At least then he'd know.

Still, she said nothing.

Chapter Two

Karla Jenkins tried to find the right words and put them in the right order. Cache Bryant had just asked her out. Right out loud. She'd noticed that they'd been flirting on and off for a few months now, and he was brilliant with a guitar in his hands.

And with these cows, as she'd never seen a cow just lie right down and let a human curl into it. But two of his had done exactly that, and she couldn't wait to report back to Scarlett.

"It's fine," Cache said. "Never mind." He turned and started walking away, everything in Karla desperate to call him back. But she just watched as he moved over to a different cow and started talking to it too, in the same human-like way he had Flower.

"Flower," she whispered, stroking her hand down the cow's hide again. "How do I tell him?" She wanted to go out with him, and she was flattered he'd asked. But she had so many things she *didn't* want to talk about. Mistakes from her past. And didn't people talk about their past when they started dating?

Karla hadn't been in the game for a while, but she thought she still knew the rules. And Cache would want to know about her, and she'd have to tell him things if she wanted to keep him in her life.

The two sides of herself went to war, and she honestly had no idea which one would win. The man—the ridiculously handsome cowboy—in question glanced over to her, and Karla still stood there, unsure about what to do.

She wasn't sure if her heart could take another battering. "Maybe he'll be gentle with your heart," she whispered to herself. Yeah, and maybe he could train these cows to fly. She didn't think so, but she needed to explain.

She stepped around the legs of the cow and headed toward him. "Cache," she said just as he snuggled into the side of a cow.

"Come join me," he said. "I want them to be able to tolerate two people."

"Cache," she repeated, and he gestured for her to come over.

She did, stepping between the hooves and sitting on the ground next to Cache. Their eyes met, and he was so, so handsome. Her breath caught in her throat, and she found herself diving all the way into his blue, blue eyes.

"Good girl, Cookie," he said, patting the cow.

"Do you have names for all of them?" she asked.

"Just a few," he said. "The several I've been working with on the cuddling."

"How do you pick them?"

"Well, all the cows are girls," he said. "So I just call them whatever. Daisy or Flower. Bluebell. Floral varieties are popular, obviously." He put that delightful smile on his face, and Karla's heart started bobbing somewhere in the back of her throat.

They sat in silence for a minute, and Karla decided maybe she could be honest with him. "Cache, I want to go out with you."

He turned his head and looked at her. "Are you sure?"

"Of course I'm sure. I just...." She gazed at the horizon. "This might sound stupid, but I don't want to be the talk of the ranch if we start seeing each other."

"Is that what would happen?" Cache asked, his phone buzzing.

"Possibly, and I—I'm a pretty private person."

"It's okay," Cache said, getting to his feet. "I have to get over to Piggy Paradise. I'll see you later, okay?" He didn't wait for Karla to say anything before he dashed off.

She stayed against the cow's side and gazed up into the cloudless California sky. She wanted to pray for help, but she didn't quite know how. She'd tried that before anyway, and nothing much had come from it.

She'd still lost her job. Her husband. Her baby.

The pain that always came when she allowed this

particular box to open sliced through her. She'd gotten a new job. A better job. She loved Last Chance Ranch, and it had come with the cabin that had allowed her to truly get a new start on her life.

She didn't want the husband anymore, and that really was a problem. Jackson had been terrible for her from the beginning, and she'd been a fool to think a baby could fix their broken marriage.

In the end, she'd lost both, and most of her life felt like a waste. She'd managed to put together a few pieces, but it had come at a high price. A vow that she didn't need a man in her life, something she'd kept since the divorce had been finalized five years ago.

Could she break that vow now? For a cheerful cowboy with the best eyes she'd ever seen?

She sighed as she got up too. "Thanks for the cuddle, Cookie."

LATER THAT DAY, Karla sat at her desk in her office, which was really the second bedroom in the cabin on the edge of the homestead's backyard. She hadn't made lunch for the ranch workers that day. She'd hardly gotten any work done either.

All she'd been able to do was sit at the desk and stare as she thought about Cache Bryant and his dinner invitation.

He'd taken it off the table and never really put it back on before running off to do his job. She had his phone number. She could call him. But she had no idea what to say.

"Focus," she muttered to herself, and she looked down at her computer. She was supposed to be putting up next month's goat yoga schedule, and she couldn't seem to get it done.

After that, she needed to confirm with Forever Friends about the Fourth of July picnic and adoption event, taking place in a couple of months. That event should be highly publicized around the ranch and through the Forever Friends organization, and Karla had a meeting the following day that would take her down to the offices in LA.

Anxiety hit her at having to return to the city. All those memories. All those people. But she pushed aside the panic and picked up her phone to text Vicky, the only friend she had left from her previous life.

Still on for lunch tomorrow?

Yes! Vic's text came back almost immediately. Karla smiled at her device as they confirmed their location and time. Then Karla would drive back to the ranch, back to this small cabin, back to this simpler, easier life.

Karla loved this life, but she'd started to feel like it was hollow. She was a shell, with nothing of substance inside.

And her thoughts went back to Cache again. Wondering if he could provide some sort of fulfillment for her, Karla once again stalled in her work. Could she really find out? She'd heard all of the love stories here on the ranch—and if he didn't think they'd be the source of all gossip if they even so much as glanced at each other with a playful glint in their eyes, he was sorely mistaken—and she didn't want to feel like she couldn't be here if she and Cache started something and broke up.

She didn't need to repeat what had happened in the city.

Keep it a secret.

Words that Scarlett had said to her that morning, regarding the cow cuddling Cache had been doing in the pasture right across the lane from her cabin. Apparently, he'd been working with his cows for a long time, and she hadn't known.

But now, her brain was suggesting she keep her relationship with Cache a secret. She scoffed out loud. There was *no* relationship with Cache.

"Yet," she muttered under her breath. And maybe if she could get him to ask her to dinner again, she could suggest they go, sure. But that no one else could know.

Satisfied with that solution, Karla was finally able to get some work done.

"Girl, you have lost weight," Vic said when Karla walked into the restaurant where they'd agreed to meet for lunch.

She scoffed. "I have not." She hugged her friend. "If anything, I've gained ten pounds feeding everyone on the ranch."

"You were always a genius with feeding large groups." Vic nodded to the hostess, and she grabbed two menus and took them back to a table. "I miss that about you around the office."

Karla put a smile on her face and nodded. "I don't miss much about the city," she said. "I can handle coming for a meeting, but I don't want to live or work here." And not only because she might run into Jackson.

"How'd the meeting go?" Vic asked, getting situated on the bench across from Karla. "You're working with that animal sanctuary, right?"

"Right," Karla said. "It went great. I love the people there. They have a real passion for saving abandoned or injured animals."

Vic smiled and nodded, and Karla needed to change the subject. She loved her friend, but Vic didn't understand how Karla could leave the city and be happy. Sometimes Karla couldn't believe it either.

"So there's a new band I'm into," Karla said, and Vic's face lit up. She enjoyed lunch with her friend, but she didn't ask any questions about Karla's life. Didn't ask if she was seeing anyone new, or had made any friends, or if she liked the cabin she'd been living in for almost a year.

As she hugged her BFF good-bye, Karla couldn't help but think that the relationship had turned...hollow. Just like everything else in her life.

She kept the radio off as she drove back to Last Chance Ranch, hoping some inspiration would strike her. Or maybe lightning. At this point, Karla would take almost anything.

As she drove up the dirt road to the ranch, she noticed someone had put a pair of bunny ears on the robot that stood sentinel at the entrance. She smiled at them, a little ray of hope in her otherwise dreary existence.

She wasn't sure why they were there, as Easter had come and gone last month. But it didn't matter. Karla drove down the road to the back of her cabin, parked, and got out, the bunny ears reminding her that even the simplest of things mattered.

She mattered.

To who, she wasn't sure, but she could start with Scarlett and Hudson. They depended on her to get promotional activities ready for the ranch. Maintain the website. Feed the people on the ranch.

They needed her.

Even if God had abandoned her. Even if Jackson had left in the middle of the night. Even if she'd walked into her job one morning and walked out an hour later, all her stuff in a pathetic, brown box.

Her phone chimed, and she pulled it out of her purse to check it.

Hey, Karla, Cache had texted. *Do you have a sec? I need to talk to you about something.*

A smile pulled at the corners of her mouth.

Cache needed her, too.

Chapter Three

Cache glared at Scarlett, but he'd sent the text. "She had a meeting in the city," he said, hating himself a little for even knowing Karla's schedule. "She won't be back yet."

"I just saw her pull up," Hudson said without looking up from his phone.

"Why are you being weird about this?" Scarlett asked, pure curiosity on her face. "You've worked here for years, and you're never anything but cheerful and fun."

"Okay," Cache said with more dryness in his voice than a desert. He was not always cheerful and fun. Take right now, for instance.

"Seriously," Scarlett said, moving into the kitchen and starting to load the dishwasher with their breakfast dishes.

Cache sighed even as his phone went off. "She said sure. Should I have her come here?"

"No," Scarlett said. "Meet her at her place. She has an office." She finished with the dishes and faced him again. "What's up with you and her?"

"Nothing," Cache said, and that was the absolute truth.

"That's the problem, dear," Hudson said, still tapping on his phone. "I have to go. My dad wants me to do help him with something at the stables tonight. I'm okay to go?"

"Yes, go," Scarlett said, and Hudson kissed her quick and walked out the front door, leaving her with Cache. And a load of questions in her eyes. "Is he right?"

"No," Cache said. "Yes. I don't know." He glanced away, the darkness he'd been feeling lately starting to crowd into his soul. He heaved a big breath, because Scarlett was still staring at him. "I asked her out. She said no."

Scarlett's eyebrows shot toward the sky. "She did?"

"I think so."

"You think so?"

Now that Cache thought about it, she hadn't really answered at all. "She sort of just laid there, all cuddled up to the cow. She never really said."

"Maybe you caught her off-guard."

"You mean the way you did to me when you told her about the cow cuddling and didn't mention it to me?" He glared at his boss, not really angry, but wishing he'd been able to reveal his cow cuddling methods in a different way.

"Yeah," Scarlett said, shrugging. "Like that. Look, just

go talk to her about it. I want this program up and running this summer. I feel like we're wasting money with it."

She hadn't been out to the pasture once, so she wouldn't even know. But Cache didn't say that. He just pulled out his phone and texted Karla that he could come to her place and her earliest convenience.

I'm free now, she said. *Come on over.*

He'd always been attracted to her positivity. Her quick smile. The joy she radiated as she stood behind the table and served hundreds of people without ever running out of food. How she said he could come over right then, after she'd been to meetings and driven through city traffic.

How anyone lived in LA was beyond him. He could barely stomach the people in Pasadena, and Last Chance Ranch itself had a hundred people who came to work there each day. He looked at Scarlett again, marveling at how she'd grown this place in just a few years. He'd come on pretty early in the process, before the volunteer house was done, before the administration buildings, before the full-time veterinary clinic.

He was happy for all the help, as the workload he and the other cowboys had shouldered in the beginning was back-breaking. He liked the sense of family and cama-raderie he had with the other men in the Community, but there were a lot of faces he didn't know on the ranch these days.

And more to come, if Scarlett got her way and cow

cuddling opened up this summer. And Scarlett would get her way.

"Fine," Cache said, though he wasn't really angry with her. "I'm headed over there now."

"Good," Scarlett said. "Keep me updated."

Cache had just opened the back door when she added, "And Cache, maybe ask her out again? Give her time to answer."

"Sure." He'd given her plenty of time to answer last time, and she'd just stared at him. He wasn't going to further humiliate himself for no reason. The woman knew he was interested. *She* could ask *him* this time.

He crossed the lawn and knocked on the door, hearing Karla call out, "Come on in," a moment later.

He went on in, getting a blast of cinnamon and sugar with only one step inside her house. Her cabin was the same layout as Gramps's, but hers was much cleaner, with freshly painted walls and actual countertops that weren't covered with stuff.

She wasn't there, and Cache wasn't going to go traipsing down the hall. Karla appeared a few seconds later, adjusting the hem on her T-shirt as if she'd just changed. Cache's mouth went dry at the sight of her wearing a tight, tight, tight pair of jeans and that sky blue T-shirt with the California flag on it.

"Hey," she said with a smile. "I put some snickerdoodles in the oven a few minutes ago. Can't have a meeting without cookies."

"Actually," he said. "You can. I've been in plenty of meetings without cookies."

Karla laughed, and Cache wished it didn't make his heartbeat ricochet around inside his chest.

"How did you know this would be a meeting?" he asked next, moving cautiously into the kitchen area with her. She had a long bar that ran from the living room toward the kitchen sink, and he kept that between them.

"I suspected," she said. "Plus, I need cookies after my day today." She threw him a weary look, and Cache knew he shouldn't have asked her to meet right then. But Scarlett wouldn't leave the issue alone.

"We can do this another day," he said.

"It's about the cow cuddling, right?" She donned a pair of oven mitts and bent over to check the cookies.

Cache didn't mean to stare, but she had curves in all the right places, and he couldn't look away. Her very presence revved him up, and he didn't want to be calmed down.

"Yes," he said, his voice cracking. He cleared his throat, but it was still so dry. "The cow cuddling."

"I'm going to need you to explain it to me," she said. "I'm supposed to start on a website, and we'll need to talk about length of sessions, price, how many people, time of day, all of it."

All stuff Cache hadn't thought about at all. "I've been really focused on training the cows to lie down and stay there while people touch them," he said. "It's not natural for them."

"Why would someone want to do this?" Karla asked, using a spatula to move the cookies from the tray to a cooling rack. She didn't put any more cookies in to bake and moved the rack to the island where Cache stood. "Eat."

He took a cookie, the flakiness of it making his mouth water. Or maybe that was all the sugar and cinnamon filling his nose. Or the gorgeous woman in front of him. She was definitely the reason for his fantasies springing to life.

"Apparently, people need a city escape," he said. "Get back to their roots. Experience nature without having to camp or drive too far."

"Last Chance Ranch is perfect for that," she said. "We're five minutes up the road."

"And a lot of people already know about us from the goat yoga," he added.

"So this will go on the front page of the ranch's website," she said. "And we need to build a site of its own." She glanced at him. "Right?"

"I would think so," he said. "Or just a page on the ranch's site." He honestly had no idea.

"Goat yoga has its own," she said. "I'll ask Scarlett about it, but we want people to be able to find us when they search. If it's too buried...." She shook her head and picked up a pen. Scrawling notes on a tall pad of paper, she took a bite of her cookie.

Cache watched her chew, a few grains of sugar stuck to her lips. He wanted to kiss it off, and instant heat flooded his body.

She turned you down, bro, he told himself. *Do not ask her out again.*

He picked up a cookie and ate half of it in one bite, just so he wouldn't have to talk should she ask him something.

She finished writing and looked up at him. Their eyes met, and Cache only continued to breathe and blink because they were involuntary functions. Karla straightened, something firing in her blue eyes he'd seen a time or two before. They'd flirted a few times since she'd come to the ranch, and she'd worn this playfulness several times over the months.

No wonder Cache thought she was interested in him. She *looked* interested in him.

She flinched and focused back on her notepad. "How much would you charge for this?"

He swallowed the cookie and wiped his mouth. "A lot. I think the article I read was charging people three hundred dollars for a couple of hours. It was a couple's session too."

"So one-fifty for two hours, per person."

"Yeah," he said. "Sounds right."

"How many people do you need to run the program?"

"Uh." Cache didn't know what she meant. "I guess just me?"

"You're going to do all of the sessions?"

"Scarlett wants this up and going this summer," he said. "The cows only respond to me. I don't have time to train someone." He didn't even want to train someone. He felt extremely protective of his cattle, as they were all he had left from the family dairy farm in Nevada. He'd watched Carson Chatworth get over the loss of his ranch in Montana, but he'd found himself a wife pretty soon after that, and Cache felt certain Adele had helped a lot in that transition.

Cache still felt like he was transitioning.

Exhaustion pulled through him, and he still had band practice that night.

"I'll talk to Scarlett," Karla said, and that only added fuel to the simmering anger in Carson's gut.

"No," he said, drawing Karla's attention. Her eyes widened, and she straightened again. "I get to decide who works with my cows. Not Scarlett. We'll have to do the sessions when I'm available."

"And when would that be?" Karla asked coolly.

Cache clenched his teeth. "I don't know. I'll look at my schedule and let you know." He reached into his pocket and pulled out his phone. "Sorry, Karla, I have to go." No one had texted him, but she didn't need to know that. "I have band practice tonight."

Not a lie. He could stay for a lot longer, and maybe if

they cuddled on the couch, her giggling as he told her what had happened with the llamas that afternoon, he would stay.

But the tension in her cabin was enough to make his teeth ache, and he couldn't stand to be there for another moment.

"Thanks for the cookies." He started for the front door, hoping the air outside wouldn't be so full of Karla.

"Cache," she called after him.

He turned with his hand on the doorknob. "Yeah?"

She opened her mouth to say something, but she just stood there. Cache really wasn't in the mood for this, and he twisted the knob.

"It was good to see you," she finally said, and he gave her the best smile he could. It was tight and sat wrong on his face, but he ducked outside a moment later and she couldn't see him.

It was good to see you. Her words echoed in his ears, giving him false hope. He didn't care. False hope was better than none at all.

Chapter Four

Karla bustled down the road to Gramps's, where the two pans of pizza casserole should be coming out of the oven any minute. Adele would take the casseroles out at her place, and then Karla just had to make it back to hers. Cover everything with tin foil. Put in six more trays.

Lunch would be ready on time, and she smiled to herself.

Yes, she spent a crazy amount of time making lunch for hundreds of people. But not everyone came, especially the volunteers, who were the bulk of the people who came to Last Chance Ranch every day.

Karla honestly hadn't planned to make lunch today. She had several action items that needed to be started from her meeting yesterday, and this whole cow cuddling thing to wrap her mind around.

But she wanted to see Cache again. Plain and simple, he was the reason she'd gotten up at six-thirty and started boiling water for penne. She couldn't admit that to anyone, and making lunch for the cowboys was something she did regularly. No one would think it out of the ordinary, and she'd get to see Cache.

"Hey, Gramps," she said as she went inside his cabin. She didn't knock anymore, and the old man smiled at her.

"Karla, the oven hasn't gone off yet."

"It will," she said, stepping around a couple of trash bags. She'd take those out after lunch too. "You're coming for lunch, right?"

"Oh, Hudson will come get me, I'm sure," Gramps said. Hound lifted his head from Gramps's feet, probably at the sound of his master's name.

Karla opened the oven and checked the casseroles. Nice and cheesy and bubbly. She pulled one out and replaced it with a cold one. Repeating the action, she had two more dishes in and two out. After removing the oven mitts, she covered the finished casseroles in tin foil and wiped her hair out of her eyes with a big sigh. "Thanks for letting me use your oven, Gramps."

"Yes, yes," he said, and Karla grinned at him.

"Okay, lunch in an hour or so." She started for the back door again, unsurprised when Hudson's dog came with her. "I'm going to take him, okay?"

"He needs to get out," Gramps said, standing. Karla hurried back to help him, as he often needed just a few seconds to stabilize on his feet. "I'm going to come sit in the shade."

"All right," she said, employing her patience. It would take three times as long to get back to her place with Gramps and get him set up in the shade of her cabin until lunchtime. *It's fine*, she told herself. She didn't need to rush all over the place, even if she'd chosen a hard dish to feed eighty people.

The real rush would come when she had to make the garlic bread. But she knew a trick—butter the long French loaves first. Cut second. Broil third. She'd used to do the broiling second, and then she was dealing with hot, sizzling garlic butter as she tried to cut the loaf into pieces.

But not today. Today, she'd have that hot, buttery bread on the table when the cowboys showed up.

"How's the family?" Gramps asked, taking the back steps one by one.

"Good," Karla said. "Lisa just got engaged, so I'll be headed back east for her wedding."

"That's great," Gramps said. "To that Harlow fellow?"

"That's right," Karla said with a big smile at Gramps's use of the word fellow. "They haven't set a date yet, but you know how particular Lisa can be."

Gramps had actually never met Karla's younger sister —either of them. But she'd told him about her family back in Virginia, and he'd told her story after story from his childhood, his time here on the ranch raising his family, and dozens of other things.

31

Karla loved Gramps, and spending time with him and helping him made her feel less useless in the world. And less guilty about leaving her family when she married Jackson and they moved across the country to California.

After the divorce, Karla had embraced the shame and decided to stay out west. Her mother hadn't quite understood, but Wendy, Karla's other sister, had provided a sufficient distraction by getting engaged and then married.

That event had brought Karla home, and that had been enough for her mother. She tried to get to Virginia at least once each year, and she said, "Wendy just had a baby."

"Yes, a boy, like Sawyer and Jeri."

Karla kept her arm looped through Gramps's as they stepped down the dirt road to her place. "Yep," she said. "So I'll probably go visit sometime soon. Maybe in the fall." She was musing now, and she needed to check her calendar and decide on dates. Her mom would like that, and maybe she'd get to help with some of Lisa's wedding prep.

"Here you go, Gramps," she said, delivering him to the rocking chair on her front porch. The sun would stay out of his way until lunchtime, and then he'd go sit under the tents with everyone else. "I have to get back to work, okay? Yell if you need me."

"I'll be fine," he said, already rocking back and forth.

Karla gave him a smile, fondness moving through her. She wondered who would take care of her when she was old like Gramps, but she pushed the thought away. She couldn't dwell on negative things. Not today.

She'd already texted everyone about lunch, and back inside her cabin, she got the two casserole pans out of the oven and put that last two in. Then she set to work on the final piece of the meal. Salad. It wasn't hard to open all the bags and dump them in the huge metal bowl she'd brought with her from the city.

She chopped cucumbers, tossed in a couple of containers of grape tomatoes, opened three bags of croutons, and set four bottles of ranch dressing on the counter.

Pausing, she took stock of the meal. "Almost there," she said, turning her attention to making the garlic butter for the bread.

Precisely when she said lunch would be served, lunch was served. The cowboys and ranch hands and volunteers came in shifts. She liked it, actually, because then she didn't have to worry about long lines or nowhere to sit on the tables under the tent.

Today, she'd served three pans of pizza casserole—with all that ooey gooey cheese, sausage, pepperoni, and saucy penne pasta—before Cache showed up.

Her heart ba-bumped in her chest irregularly, and she tried to cover it with a smile. "Hey, there," she said as he picked up a plate and bypassed the green stuff. She didn't take it personally. Not a lot of the men went straight for the salad.

"Hey." He smiled at her, his usual cheerful self back.

He really did project sunshine from his soul, and Karla had always been drawn to his optimism and bright charm.

"In the stables this afternoon?" she asked. "Or over in the Canine Club?" She scooped a big spoonful of casserole onto his plate.

"Stables," he said. "I'm on equipment duty."

"Maybe I'll come see Blade." She looked up at him, hoping he heard more than that. Hoping she could tell him she'd love to go to dinner with him. Hoping she hadn't messed up by simply staring at him the other morning.

"Sure," he said. "I'll put him out in the corral. He's been inside a lot lately."

"Bad hip," they said together, and Karla grinned at him. That sparking, wonderful moment lasted for a few seconds, and then two more cowboys arrived.

"Finer Diner this weekend," Lance Longcomb said. "Right, Cache?"

Cache tore his gaze from Karla's and looked at his band mates, Lance and Dave. "Right. Let's make sure we remind Sawyer. I haven't seen him around much."

Dave picked up a plate and Karla scooped noodles and cheese and meat onto it. "Thank you, Karla." He smiled at her too, nudging Cache to move already. Karla flicked one more glance at him and then focused on feeding the men who'd gotten in line.

Her moment with Cache was over, but she caught him watching her a couple of times while she continued to serve and he ate lunch with his friends. He didn't stop by to say thank you or good-bye, and a twist of longing for him hit her.

She didn't know what to do with it. She'd had enough emotional turmoil and pain from a broken, brutal relationship to last a lifetime.

She'd escaped that life, and she'd vowed never to go back.

Cache is not Jackson, she told herself as she started putting leftovers in disposable containers. She had ten of them, and she'd text a select group of cowboys who lived here on the ranch to come get what they wanted. Cache included.

She slipped one of the containers into her cabin, leaving only nine sitting in the shade. She texted the men, including Cache, about the leftovers, and then texted him separately.

I kept some food for you in my cabin.

Thanks! he texted back.

Karla stared at her phone. Maybe she could just ask him to dinner through this. He'd been brave and asked her right to her face. But she wasn't as brave as him.

I'd love to go to dinner with you. She typed the words out and looked at them, making sure every letter was in the right place.

Before she could chicken out, she hit *send.*

And I'd love to know when you're playing at Finer Diner. Maybe I could come watch.

If he didn't know she was interested after those two texts, he really wasn't as bright as she'd thought.

She'd splashed cold water on her face and scrubbed her hands and arms up to her elbows before her phone made a peep. Drying off quickly, she glanced at her device. But the screen darkened before she could read Cache's response.

With still damp fingers and a trembling heart, Karla swiped open the conversation.

Let's talk when you come to the stables. I'm here all afternoon.

"Hey, he didn't say no," Karla said to her empty cabin. "And he didn't stare at you, dumbfounded either."

She couldn't believe she'd done that to him. But she couldn't rewind time and fix it. Just like she couldn't make the days go backward to rectify any of the mistakes she'd made in her marriage, and she couldn't get back the precious few months she'd been pregnant.

Her heart wailed now, as Karla had opened a box she'd swore she'd never even think about again.

"I'm sorry," she whispered, but whether that was to Jackson, herself, or God, she wasn't sure. She just knew she couldn't keep living in this hollow shell. Something had to change. She could only hope the transformation wouldn't be too painful.

"Please, Lord," she whispered, but her faith had grown cold years ago and she couldn't articulate much more than that. Her feeble attempt brought warmth to her soul, and she drew in a deep breath.

She'd done hard things before. She could talk to Cache Bryant and make sure he knew she hadn't meant to hurt him.

Chapter Five

Cache took inventory of the equipment in the stables, weeding out any rope that wasn't usable anymore. He cleaned up all the tools and made sure they were where they were supposed to be. He refilled the oats and feed, and had just moved onto tack when someone entered the building.

It could've been anyone, but he knew instantly it was Karla. His pulse skipped, but he kept his whistling going as if he didn't know she'd really come to see him. Under the ruse of wanting to see Blade, of course. But Cache wasn't dim, and he'd felt something between them at lunch.

He'd been feeling it for months. Surely she had too.

So he just needed to figure out what was going on with her. Then maybe he'd be able to sleep at night. Maybe he'd be able to think about something besides holding her hand. Maybe, maybe, maybe.

"Hey," she said, and Cache jumped, a smile already crossing his face.

"Hey." He held a saddle between them, because he noticed how nervous she looked.

"I'm really sorry," she blurted. "I just...wasn't expecting you to ask me to dinner the other day, and I sort of blanked."

Cache appreciated the apology, but he knew there was more going on with her. He wanted to know what it was. Wanted to know everything about her. "It's okay," he said.

"I'd like to go to dinner with you." She raised her chin a fraction of an inch, almost daring him to turn her down.

"I'd like that too," he said, ducking his head as heat rushed into his face. "We've got band practice again on Friday, because we're playing at the diner on Saturday."

"I'll come," she said, stepping closer to him. She wore no makeup, and her hair fell over her shoulders in beautiful waves of ripened grain. "Cache, I—" She didn't continue, and Cache wondered if he just needed to do what Scarlett had advised. Give her time to respond.

"There's something going on with you," he said. "I'm— I want to know what."

She started nodding, her hands twisting together.

"You don't need to be nervous," he said gently. "It's just me. Cache. We've been friends for ten months."

She nodded and swallowed, but she still looked like he

was a phantom she needed to banish in the next ten seconds.

"An old boyfriend?" he asked, and tears filled her eyes. Cache couldn't have that. He set the saddle aside and drew Karla into his arms. Relief and wonder filled him, and he pressed his eyes closed at the feel of her body next to his. "Hey," he whispered. "It's okay. You don't have to tell me anything you don't want to. Okay?"

She nodded against his chest, and her grip around him stayed tight and strong. So he just held her close, praying that she could find whatever relief she needed from this turmoil inside her.

He held her until she stepped back, and then he let her go. "I just—I swore I'd never have another man in my life." She swiped at her face, but her eyes were still lovely and bright when she looked at him.

"I'm sorry for whatever happened," he said, deciding to go with his own pathetic love life. "I grew up on that dairy farm in Nevada, right? Well, there weren't a lot of girls out there, let me tell you." He flashed her a smile and turned to find the saddle oil. He might as well work while they talked. Hudson wouldn't like him using his daylight hours to flirt anyway.

"So there was this one girl I *really* liked. Her name was Lisa."

"That's my sister's name," Karla said.

Cache grinned. "So that'll make this interesting. Anyway, I liked her a lot. Like, a lot-a lot. She had all this blonde hair, and these blue eyes, and she could ride a horse like no one I'd ever seen." He was aware that he'd basically just described Karla, and maybe Cache had a weakness for blondes. He wasn't sure.

"Anyway, I asked her to go to the fair with me, and we met there. Only she didn't think we were there together. She thought I'd just asked if she'd be there. Turned out, she was sweet on my brother, and she spent the whole night with him." Cache chuckled and shook his head. "I felt like such an idiot." He moved the polishing rag around and around, getting all the creases in the leather.

"Did she and Leo last?"

"Nope," Cache said. "Dated for a summer, and then she broke up with him." Cache hung the saddle back on the wall and moved to the next one. "Honestly, Karla, I haven't dated a whole lot in my life." Embarrassment squirreled through him. "I've had maybe four or five women I'd call a girlfriend. Hardly anything serious."

He swallowed and told himself to stop talking. He kept his head down and worked, hoping she'd say something now.

"I was married for five years."

Cache whipped his attention to her, his eyes widening. He searched her face, trying to find out if the marriage was good, bad, ugly, or what. Had her husband died? Did she have kids? Why had he never seen them? Suspected this?

She fiddled with the end of some reins that were

hanging on the wall. "His name was Jackson. We met in Virginia, fell in love, and got married. He got a job out here shortly after that, and we moved across the country."

Cache couldn't work and listen at the same time. Married. He tried to get over the shock of it. Karla was his age—thirty-nine. Of course she'd had time in her past life to get married.

"Things went bad after about the first year," she said quietly. "He couldn't hold a job, so I went to work. I mean, I was working anyway, but I started moving up in my firm." She pressed her lips together into a thin, white line. "But, it didn't work out. We had...too many problems. A lot of problems, and money was only one of them." She smiled, but it was weak and pained, and Cache had the distinct impression to pull her right back into his arms and tell her everything was okay now.

"How long ago?" he asked.

She swiped at her eyes again and straightened her shoulders. "Five years," she said. "He's still in the state, somewhere."

"No kids?"

Something flashed through her eyes, and she shook her head no. "I told myself I wouldn't go through that again."

Cache nodded, realizing she had a much more complicated past to navigate than he did. He couldn't help seizing onto the fact that she and her first husband had had money problems. Cache himself didn't have much in the way of money, and how could he ever provide for a woman like Karla? A family?

He tamped down the inadequate feelings. They hadn't even gone to dinner yet. Maybe now they wouldn't.

"Listen, we don't—" He cut off when her hand touched his. Her fingers sneaked between his, sending warmth and light and fireworks through his whole system. He stared at their joined hands before lifting his eyes to hers.

"Maybe dinner on Monday night?" she whispered, and Cache saw the hope in her eyes. No, he didn't know what the future held. But he could hope for a good one, couldn't he?

"Dinner on Monday night," he echoed.

Karla smiled, this time the gesture wasn't full of pain from the past. "Great. Now, I really do want to see Blade."

CACHE FIDDLED with the strings on his guitar, knowing Lance would take it from him in a minute. He really should leave them alone, as they'd already tuned together. But Cache always had all this pent-up energy before a gig.

Not only that, he'd caught sight of Karla slipping through the door just a moment ago. Their eyes hadn't met. She hadn't come to the front, almost like she wanted to stay out of sight. Didn't want anyone to see her.

His phone buzzed in his back pocket, and he reached for it.

Good luck! Karla had texted. *You'll be brilliant.*

He smiled and shoved his phone in his pocket again as Lance took his guitar. "You've messed it all up," he said, turning the tuning pegs and strumming. "I don't know why you do this."

"Because you'll fix it for me," Cache said, stepping over to the doorway to find the diner was packed. Dave didn't seem to care at all as his fingers flew across the screen of his phone. Probably texting Sissy. They were a cute couple, and Cache had been surprised to learn that they'd dated and been engaged before.

It seemed like everyone around him was better than him. Further along in their lives, their career, the financial future than he was. Since talking to Karla, he'd decided that the Last Chance Cowboys needed more gigs. He'd always saved his band money—not that it was much—and maybe he could get a little nest egg going before he confessed to Karla that he basically lived hand-to-mouth and had nothing to offer her.

Helplessness filled him, and he really didn't have time for it. On the tiny stage in the restaurant, the manager got behind the mic.

"Guitar," he said, and Lance handed it back to him. "This is it, guys. We're on in a minute." As if they didn't know. Couldn't hear the manager introducing them.

Dave finally put his phone away and rolled his shoulders, about all he ever did to be ready for a gig. Sawyer grinned at Cache, who couldn't help but feel the electricity and energy of the crowd.

That high would ride with him for days, and he loved how every performance was different based on the crowd.

"The Last Chance Cowboys," the manager practically yelled, and Dave led the way out of the back room where they'd been warming up and getting ready to take the stage. Cache honestly didn't mind not being the front guy. He was an excellent guitar player, and he knew it.

"Hey, everyone," Dave said into the mic, already on his game. "We know you're here to eat, but we hope you'll enjoy the entertainment as well." He looked around at everyone, getting a nod from Lance behind the drums, and they launched into their first song.

Cache saw the surprise on some of the patron's faces. He'd eaten at Finer Diner lots of times since coming to Last Chance Ranch, and some of the entertainment was lackluster, to say the least.

As they played through their set of eight songs, people clapped along. A few got up to dance in the small space in front of the stage. Cache tried not to focus all of his attention on Karla, but she'd gotten a table way over in the corner, and she'd put a hat over her gorgeous, wavy hair.

She didn't want to be seen there. He wondered what that was about, and he'd definitely be asking her later. But for right now, he just lived in the moment, playing guitar and singing backup with his band.

Chapter Six

Karla had heard Cache's band play before. They were good. Really good. She couldn't look at anyone but him, and he was completely in his element up there. So sexy in those jeans and cowboy boots, his guitar slung over those broad shoulders.

Karla smiled the whole time he was on stage, and as soon as their set ended, she threw cash on her table and headed for the door.

She'd forgotten to tell him that she'd like to keep their budding relationship a secret. Not necessarily a secret, but she didn't want rumors flying around the ranch the way they already were about Dave and Sissy. She didn't need anyone talking about her. She didn't need to explain anything to Scarlett, or Amber, or Adele.

In the safety of her car, she texted Cache again. *You*

were so great. She wanted to add how handsome he was, how talented, but she wasn't sure if they were to that level in their relationship yet.

She'd come to see him play, and that spoke for itself. So she sent the message as-is and headed back to the ranch. She wondered if he'd go out with his friends afterward. Maybe stay at the diner and eat.

She found herself wanting to see him, hold his hand, and tell him all she thought of him while the stars shone overhead. When she pulled her phone out to ask him if maybe he'd meet her somewhere on the ranch, she remembered she'd put her phone on silent during the concert.

He'd texted a few times and called once.

Thanks, he'd said. *You ran out.*

Want to go get ice cream with us?

You must be home already. Talk later.

Exactly what she feared would happen had almost happened. He wanted her to go out with his band—practically announcing that they were together.

But were they together?

Karla's confusion swept through her, and she decided to call Cache. "Hey," she said when he answered. "Sorry, I put my phone on silent." She moved to the back porch, hoping the sky would absorb some of the seriousness of this conversation.

"It's fine," he said loudly, clearly still out with everyone.

"Look," she said. "I'll be really quick. I...well, I don't want us to be public."

"Be public?" Something scratched on his end of the line, and it became clear that he was moving as the noise died down and it was just his voice when he said, "I don't know what you mean."

"I don't want everyone on the ranch to know we're seeing each other," she said. "I'd like to keep anything we have between us in the shadows."

"Okay," Cache said slowly. "Why?"

"I don't know." Karla sighed. "I just think maybe I've been the topic of enough gossip in my lifetime." She hadn't told him everything about her past. Not even close. "And I just want...I just want us to be able to be us. And once all the women around here know, I'll have to answer all these questions, and I just don't want to do that."

"Us to be us," he repeated. "Where are you right now?"

"The ranch."

A beat of silence passed until he said, "I want to see you," in a low voice, as if someone had just come up to him and he didn't want them to overhear.

"Then come see me," she said, feeling flirtatious and reckless at the same time.

He chuckled. "I might need a few minutes," he said. "If I bolt now, everyone will know there's a woman. Wouldn't be keeping the secret."

"You're okay with us keeping things on the down-low?"

"Karla," he said in that smooth, delicious voice he sang with. Her heart vibrated at the sound of her name in that voice. "I'm fine with whatever you want, sweetheart. I just —I just like you. I want to get to know you." His voice cracked on the last word. "Yeah. I'm fine with just keeping things between us."

Karla smiled into the darkness beyond her back porch. "Great," she said. "See you soon."

CACHE'S FOOTSTEPS crunched against the gravel road about forty-five minutes later. He had his phone's flashlight on, and he swept it up her steps and right into her eyes. "Oh, hey," he said, his voice easy and light, tinged with surprise.

"Hey, yourself." Karla smiled, glad when he lowered the light and then lowered himself onto the step beside her. "You were great tonight."

"Thank you," he said, switching off the flashlight. "I'm glad you came." His hand touched her knee, and then his fingers slipped between hers. It was dark on the ranch—so very dark—but she had a light on inside her house, and the cheery yellow light illuminated enough of his face as he turned toward her that she could see his smile.

He inched closer to her, until his shoulder touched hers, and the heat from his thigh seeped into hers.

"I was wondering something," he said.

"Just something?" Karla thought Cache should probably have a lot of questions. She may not want to answer them, but she wouldn't mind getting to know him better too.

He chuckled, the sound soft and loud at the same time. Karla glanced next door to Carson and Adele's place, but all the windows in their cabin stayed dark.

"Would you like to help me with the cow cuddling?" he asked. "Flower sure seemed to like you, and maybe we could fit more people into a session if there are two of us."

Surprise darted through Karla. "Oh, you mean help during the sessions."

"Yeah," he said. "And before that, obviously. I'd need to train you on how I've trained them, and teach you what to do if they're being stubborn cows."

She laughed softly. "Stubborn cows."

"Hey, bovines can be some of the most stubborn animals on the planet." His fingers adjusted in hers, and she liked this casual display of his feelings for her. She wanted to hold his hand forever, memorize the way his palm fit against hers, enjoy the rush of heat from his skin, all of it.

"I bet they can," she said. "I think I have time in my schedule to help with the cow cuddling. I'll talk to Scarlett to make sure."

"Sounds good." Cache fell into silence then, and Karla liked that they didn't have to stuff the space between them with words. After a minute or so, he said, "So you have a sister named Lisa. I think you've mentioned another one at some point."

"Wendy," Karla said. "They're both younger than me."

"Are they married? Nieces and nephews?"

"Wendy's married, and she just had a baby boy," Karla said. "Lisa just got engaged." She gazed out into the night, trying not to feel like a failure. "They both live in the same town where we grew up. I'll probably go visit them this fall, see the baby, help with the wedding preparations. All of that."

"You get along with them?"

"Yeah, sure," she said, looking over to him. "You're wondering why I stayed here after a divorce I still cry over when my family is all back east."

He lifted one sexy shoulder into a shrug. "I mean, maybe."

Karla had wondered the same thing. She had a marketing degree, and she could use it anywhere. Companies in Virginia would hire her, pay her, and she could be closer to her family.

"I just...feel like maybe I don't belong there," she said. "Every time I think about going back to Norfolk, it doesn't feel right."

"Hmm," he said. "I understand that."

Karla had stopped going to church five years ago, but

she felt like she still listened to her feelings. To the Lord's promptings. Her faith wasn't what it once had been, she knew that.

"Other siblings besides Leo?" she asked. "I haven't heard you mention anyone."

"Just him," Cache said. "He and my dad went to Texas when we lost the dairy farm."

"Why didn't you go with them?"

"That's a great question," he said, his head moving down slightly as he looked at the ground. "Probably because it didn't feel right. I saw this job come up here, and Scarlett said I could bring the cows. If I hadn't bought them here, we'd have had to get rid of them. Shiloh Ridge only let my dad take a certain number."

"Do you miss them?"

"Yes," he said simply. "My mother died years ago, and Leo, Dad, and I were close. We're still close, I suppose."

Karla nodded into the night, wishing it could go on forever. "So you're great on the guitar, great with animals, and you love your family. You're darn near perfect." She nudged him playfully with her shoulder.

"I'm not perfect," he said, not even a hint of a chuckle or a tease in his voice.

"I know," Karla said, feeling stupid.

"Good," he said. "Because relationships fall apart when one thinks the other is perfect."

"I thought you said you hadn't had any serious relationships."

"I haven't," he said. "But I'm thirty-nine-years-old, and I have eyes. And friends." He looked at her, and even through the darkness, she saw the earnestness in his eyes. The way he looked at her like he wanted to kiss her. "And I've seen things I don't want to happen to me."

Karla couldn't hold his gaze. She'd seen things too. Actually had things happen to her she didn't want to have happen again. She'd put a wall around her heart and built it up for five years.

And in a few days and a simple invitation to dinner, Cache had started to tear it down.

"I should get home," he said next. "I sure did like this." He leaned over, the brim of his cowboy hat bumping against her forehead. He swept it off with his free hand and pressed his lips to her cheek.

Fire started in her blood, and Karla drew in a deep breath of this man and closed her eyes.

"Cow cuddling in the morning?" he asked. "Say, ten?"

"Ten," she repeated, feeling like she was floating away on a cloud. He stood, and she opened her eyes to watch him walk away, the sound of his boots against the gravel fading until she couldn't hear it anymore.

"Oh, boy," she whispered into the night. It seemed like that wall had been blown up, and access to her heart was wide open. "What have I gotten myself into?"

But no fear came. No anxiety. Karla looked up to the stars, knowing God was there for her even if she'd stopped going to Him for every answer.

"This is okay?" she asked, and a feeling of rightness came over her.

She got up and went inside her cabin, feeling good about Cache—but not about telling him about everything in her past. After all, how did one explain about losing a baby and not feeling bad about it?

Chapter Seven

C ache rushed through his morning chores in the Canine Club, getting all the volunteer lists over to Amber by eight so walks could happen. Baths. Visits. The vet techs would be through buildings five and six that day to take care of any needs there, and Cache had everyone fed and watered by ten.

He'd have to go back after the cow cuddling session with Karla, which was fine. He liked his work with the dogs, and today, he decided to take several of his off-leash pups with him to the pasture.

"Come on, guys," he said, the six dogs that could handle leaving the Club trotting along with him. Every once in a while, a dog would get too far out of line, and Cache would whistle him back.

They all arrived at the pasture with their tongues hanging out—except Cache—and he opened the gate to let them in. After securing it, he pumped the handle on the water spigot and got it going to fill the trough.

The dogs came over and got a drink, and he said, "All right, guys. Chill." He faced the larger area of the pasture to find his bovines out about halfway. A few of them looked toward him, but several just went on eating. None of them were lying down.

Good.

"Hey," Karla said, coming toward him on the other side of the fence. She boosted herself up onto the bottom rung, and then paused. "Yeah, I can't climb over this." She laughed at herself as she got back down and continued toward the gate.

Cache opened it for her with a smile. "Morning. You look great."

She pressed into his personal space, one hand on his chest, and grinned up at him. She certainly didn't act like a woman who'd vowed to never have another man in her life. Cache had lain awake last night, trying to figure her out. Trying to determine if she was really ready to have a real relationship with him.

Because he wanted one with her. A real one. A long one. A serious one. And if she didn't want that with him, he wasn't sure what the point was of holding her hand and telling her things.

She was still withholding something from him—as evidenced by her request to keep their relationship a secret—and Cache wasn't sure how much that bothered him.

"Earth to Cache."

He blinked and came out of his thoughts. "Sorry," he said, falling back a step. He would be wise to get some answers before he went and fell for her.

"I asked if I'd worn the right thing." She gestured down her body, and Cache's eyes followed. His blood ran hotter at the sight of her curves in a pair of jeans and a T-shirt with the word SPY across the chest.

"Yeah, fine," he said, pulling his gaze back to hers. "What's with the spy shirt?"

She smiled and reached back to pull her hair into a ponytail. "I just thought it was funny. I used to have to dress up for work, so."

"You still dress up for work," he said. "Why is that? I mean, you work out of your cabin, right?"

"Yeah," she said, moving with him when he started to walk out toward the cows. "Oh, there are dogs here."

"Yeah," he said. "Sorry, you're okay with dogs, right?"

"Yeah, sure," she said. "I just didn't see them."

"They're my off-leash canines," he said. "They like to get out every once in a while, and I didn't have a volunteer for them today." On the next step, he slipped his hand into Karla's. "So why do you dress up when you don't have to?"

"Habit?" she said, and it sounded like a guess. "I have the clothes. I guess I just figure I might as well wear them."

"Well, they're nice," he said, wishing this conversation

could end. Why had he picked something so stupid to talk about?

"You like my clothes?"

"I mean...." He cut a glance at her out of the corner of his eyes. "I like that yellow blouse with the ice cream cones on it."

Karla blinked, clearly surprised. "I didn't know you paid such close attention."

Cache had given away too much. "Maybe I do."

A smile touched her mouth as she focused on the ground again, choosing carefully where to step.

"Maybe I've wanted to ask you out for a while," he said next.

"Oh."

He squeezed her hand and grinned. "Don't worry about it, Karla," he said. "You can't be good at everything." He chuckled, glad when she joined in. "So I have eleven cows I've been working with for the cuddling. I give them simple commands, and they get a small treat if they complete the task."

"You treat them?"

"Like dogs," he said, turning back. "I forgot the bag. Just a sec." He retraced his steps at double the speed to grab the bag of apples and carrots he'd hung on a fencepost that morning. After returning to Karla, he said, "Okay, got them."

The cows had started to move toward him too. "They

know what's in the bag," he said. "They're big, but they're not as dumb as people think they are."

He reached into the bag and pulled out half an apple. "I cut them in half so I can get more mileage out of them."

"You buy these?"

"There are three apple trees over in the corner of the Community," he said. "I usually don't have to buy them, but sometimes I do." He turned toward the cows. "Cows kick if they feel threatened. Don't stand behind a cow and expect it to obey you. Right in front." He squared his shoulders, thinking he should probably put together a list of rules for how to deal with cows. For Karla, sure, but especially for any guests that might come for cow cuddling.

He couldn't believe he was going to let the general public into the pasture with his cows. But maybe for three hundred dollars a couple.... He needed to talk to Karla about the money split, because he could really use the cash.

"So right in front," he repeated. "And I say 'down' when I want them to lay down. If they do it, praise and treat. Ready?" He didn't take a treat out of the bag. He'd been trying to get his animals to obey him whether they got a reward or not.

"Ready," Karla said.

Cache moved forward to the nearest cow, a huge heifer named Morning Glory. "Down," Cache commanded, and she started to lie down. It took her a few seconds to settle, and he reached into the bag and pulled out half an apple. "Good girl, Glory."

"Do all the cows have names?" Karla asked as Cache thumped the cow on her ribcage like he would pat a dog.

"The trained ones do," he said. "You'll learn them."

"You think so? They all look exactly the same to me."

"Do they?" Cache gazed around at his cows. Each one looked completely different to him, but he didn't want to admit it. "Okay, you try. Stay," he said to Glory as she shifted. "I say 'stay' to get them to stay on the ground." He looked at her, foolishness running through him. "It's not rocket science."

She beamed at him, her blue eyes beckoning him toward her. "It's great," she said, turning to another cow. "What's this one's name?"

"They're all girls," he said. "They're cows, not bulls. And that's Cookie."

"Cookie, down," Karla said, holding the apple straight out in front of her. Cookie went right down and looked up at Karla.

"Okay, wow." She turned to Cache. "That was incredible." She tossed the apple toward Cookie, but it just bounced off her head.

Cache burst out laughing and went to get the apple for his cow. "Okay, so they're not as smart as dogs," he said. "You have to *feed* them the treat."

Nervousness ran through Karla's eyes. "I don't want to get bit."

"You keep a flat palm," he said. "Shove it right in their mouth. They'll take it." Working with cattle was natural for him, but he realized it was not for Karla—and she'd already cuddled into a bovine.

The people coming for cuddling sessions would be a lot like her. Scared but excited. Impressed with a cow lying down. They'd definitely need rules for behavior and a sharp, trained eye, to make sure no one got hurt—bovines included.

"Wait. Stay," Karla said, but Cookie got right back up, completely ignoring her.

"Cookie," Cache said, facing her. "Down."

The cow went down again, and Cache gave her a carrot. "Stay." He held his hand out to her, palm forward. "I'm working on hand signals too." He surveyed his small herd in this pasture. "I think we'll probably only do two cows per sessions. One you control and one I do. That's four people."

"Six hundred bucks," she said.

"I could maybe do two or three cows," he said, glancing around. "Morning Glory is a good cow. She stays. Cookie's restless." He stepped past them and approached Bluebell. "Down," he commanded, and down she went.

"Maybe if we put them in a formation, we can be in the center and have five or six. Twelve people."

"Let's work on it," Karla said, and Cache started moving the cows into a better position. After several tries and twenty minutes, he had five cows in a semi-circular pattern, with him and Karla standing in the middle of them.

"Like that," he said, pride seeping through him. Maybe this cow cuddling thing would work. Maybe it would provide him with the extra income he needed to provide a better life for himself—and for a future wife and family.

For Karla? his mind whispered, and he couldn't help but think, *yes. For Karla.*

"Okay," he said, smiling around at his cows. "Now we cuddle."

Chapter Eight

Karla giggled as she leaned her head against Cache's bicep. A thrill ran down her spine as they held hands and laughed, all within the safety and secrecy of Cookie's huge body. Karla had never been so glad to keep something a secret, and she liked that she could hold Cache's hand in the dead of night or secluded behind a big dairy cow.

And wow, she liked this man. It was amazing how much her perspective of him had shifted since he'd invited her to dinner.

"You didn't go to church today," she said when she realized it.

Cache lifted her wrist to his lips. "Mental health day." He looked at her, sobering. "You never go to church."

Karla nodded, expecting this conversation. "I used to."

"And now?"

"Now, I'm kind of in a slump," she said. "Don't you ever feel like that? Like sometimes things are going great and you're happy and your life is exactly what you want?" She'd definitely had times like that in her life. Cache surely had too. "And sometimes, it's...not."

"And you're in a not section."

"I used to think I was," Karla said. "I don't know. I've been getting better—*feeling* better—since coming to Last Chance Ranch." She didn't know how to articulate it.

"Best place to be to feel better is at church," he said. "That's what my mom used to say, at least."

"And yet you needed a mental health day," she said, not quite understanding. "Was that from church, or something else?"

"From everything," he said, sounding tired. Karla understood that feeling too. "I mean, I always have chores. I'd have to be dead or on my way there not to go to the Canine Club to feed and water in the morning. But sometimes it's nice to not have to do anything after that." He took off his cowboy hat and closed his eyes. "Church included."

Karla watched him openly as he wasn't looking at her. He was handsome and strong, with a gorgeous jawline and his light hair cropped close, close to his scalp. She wanted to run her fingers along his face and up through that hair, see what it felt like.

Jackson had had such long hair.

She reached out, pulling back when he said, "Church isn't for the well. It's for those who need help."

"So maybe we'll go next week," she said, and he smiled.

"I'd like that."

Karla gathered her courage and reached out to him again. The first brush of her fingertips along his jaw made his eyes spring open. They met hers, and she smiled at him. He leaned into her touch, and the moment became tender and charged at the same time. Up her fingers went, and she ran them along his hair and down to the back of his neck.

"You're a great guy," she said.

"I'm broke," he whispered, anxiety entering those brilliant blue eyes.

Karla didn't know what to say. Cache had always been the cowboy with a quick smile, a fun joke, and something easy to talk about. She wasn't used to this serious cowboy, who talked about being spiritually sick, and worrying about money.

She didn't know what to say. So she just snuggled into him further, glad when his hand against her shoulder tightened to hold her in place.

"I'M GETTING WENDY," Lisa said, and she was gone before Karla could protest. She sighed as she busied herself with the hot chocolate. Yes, it was summertime, and she shouldn't be drinking something so warm. But her cabin had air conditioning, and she always made hot chocolate when she was stressed.

When big decisions needed to be made.

Her cow cuddling experience with Cache was twenty-four hours old now, and it had been wonderful. She'd spent the rest of the day in her cabin, looking up information on cow cuddling and visiting other ranch websites to see if they offered the service.

It seemed like no one did, and Karla would have to come up with her own terms, rules, and design for the addition to the Last Chance Ranch website.

Which was fine—if she could stop thinking about Cache. He hadn't said anything else after admitting he was broke, and they'd finished their session with him teaching her how to get the cows back on their feet and out to pasture.

He'd taken the dogs back to the Canine Club, and she'd gone home.

Their dinner was that night, and Karla didn't want to cancel. But she needed some reassurances from her sisters that she was doing the right thing.

"Dating?" Wendy asked instead of saying hello. "Who is he?"

Karla was glad Lisa hadn't even asked one question before going to get Wendy, who happened to be with her as they made some early plans for Lisa's wedding. The cooing of a baby came through the line, and Karla wished she could be with her sisters so badly in that moment.

"He's just a cowboy here at the ranch," Karla said.

"Just a cowboy," Lisa said, almost scoffing. "Karla, you didn't even say hello when you called. You said, 'I'm dating a guy and I need help.'"

"And you didn't let me finish," Karla said, smiling. "You ran off to get Wendy. And I do need help."

"Tell us about him," Wendy said, always the sister who could get everyone at ease. Karla probably should've called her first, but she hadn't wanted to disturb her sister and her one-month-old baby.

The microwave beeped, and Karla reached to open it. "He's handsome," she said, going on to describe Cache, ending with, "And he plays in a band, and we're going to dinner tonight, and I'm just worried I'm doing everything wrong."

"Honey," Lisa said, but it was Wendy who said, "Karla, you deserve to be happy."

"I know," she said.

"I don't think she does," Wendy said, as if she were talking to Lisa and not Karla. "She let Jackson move her across the country when she didn't want to go. She stayed with him for far too long, while he made her feel like the light turning red was her fault. She hasn't dated in—"

"Okay," Karla practically yelled, still stirring the hot chocolate. Every organ inside her pinched, and she didn't need her sister to detail every horrible thing that had happened over the years.

"It sounds like you like him," Lisa said. "And you're a smart woman, Karla."

Karla had known calling her sisters would help. She had listened to Jackson when he'd blamed her for things she couldn't control, for not moving up fast enough in her firm, for not having the right education for a particular job.

Sometimes she didn't feel smart. She didn't trust her own feelings, or what her gut said. "I didn't move across the country when I didn't want to," she said. "I've stayed, because I like it here. I'm supposed to be here."

"Okay," Wendy said. "I apologize for that."

Karla nodded to her hot chocolate. "I did stay with Jackson for too long."

"Mm," both of her sisters said. She hated the sound, but it also made her smile. They were so predictable. So steady. She felt like the only one who'd built her life on a sandy foundation. And when the winds came and the storm howled, she felt like she was about to crumble and fall into the thrashing waves, never to be seen or heard from again.

"So I'll go out with him," she said. "Because doing that makes me happy."

"He should make you happy," Wendy said. "But you can be happy without him too."

"I know," Karla said, but she wasn't sure she did. She hadn't been terribly happy since things had started downhill with Jackson. She'd lost him, lost her marriage, lost her baby. Had she been happy since then?

"Thanks, guys. Tell me how the wedding prep is going."

Lisa started talking then, and Karla sipped her hot chocolate while the three of them gabbed as if they were in the same room. As if Karla hadn't left ten years ago and only came back a couple of times a year.

It was a great conversation, and Karla said, "Tell me when to come in the fall so I can be the most helpful."

"Sometime in September," Lisa said. "We'll be doing the menu then."

"Oh, you had me at food." Karla laughed and they said their good-byes. She stayed on the couch as the silence filled the space around her. She had had moments of happiness in the five years since her life had taken a new turn.

She was getting happier by the day, she could feel that.

And she suddenly knew why she wore her professional clothes to go across the hall to her office to work.

They made her happy. She loved her yoga-slash-dress pants and her fun blouses. They made her feel feminine and cute, and she liked feeling that way. She couldn't wait to tell Cache that night when they went to dinner.

As she finished work, showered, and got dressed in her best-loved professional clothes, she felt a ray of happiness chase away some darkness in her soul.

She put on black heels with her black slacks and a dark

purple blouse that had ruffles on the sleeves. She carefully placed long, dark gray teardrop earrings in her ears, and swept just enough makeup on her face to show Cache she wanted to look good for him.

And she did.

Even if it was a secret between the two of them, she wanted him to know she liked him for real.

Fifteen minutes before he was set to pick her up, someone knocked on her front door. Assuming Cache would come to the back, Karla frowned as she went to answer the door.

Scarlett stood there, her hair in a messy bun and her face dirty. "Oh, hey," she said, scanning Karla from head to toe. "Whoa. What's going on?"

"Nothing," Karla said, her voice a little too high. "What's going on with you?"

"I was wondering if we could use your dishwasher. Ours is blowing up." She sighed like the weight of every dirty dish in the world rested on her shoulders.

Which, of course, it did. Karla couldn't even imagine what it took to manage and run this ranch, and Scarlett and Hudson did it all themselves.

"Yeah, sure," she said, stepping back. "I'll leave the door open. I'm headed out to a meeting."

"A meeting for what?" Scarlett asked.

"The cow cuddling," she said, instantly regretting it. Scarlett got that look in her eye—the one Karla had wanted to avoid. The one that said she knew this was more than a meeting, and everyone else on the ranch would know by nightfall.

"With who?"

"Cache," Karla said, seeing no reason to lie about it now. "He's asked me to work with him on it. Started teaching me the commands and stuff yesterday. We think we can get up to twelve people in per session. That's eighteen hundred dollars in two hours."

Scarlett's eyebrows stretched toward her messy hair as Hudson came across the back lawn, dishes piled in a laundry basket. "Wow."

"Right?" Karla asked. "So we're going over human behaviors tonight. He's very concerned about his cattle— and the people. He doesn't want anyone to get hurt." Karla stepped over to the built-in desk beside the hallway and picked up the folder she'd started for the cow cuddling. "I have to run," she said, thinking she'd text Cache. "We're meeting at six."

"Okay," Scarlett said, distracted now by the arrival of her husband and the dishes.

Karla escaped out the back door, her thumbs already flying over the screen of her phone. *Had to dodge Scarlett. Pick me up by Prime?*

The thought of walking a half-mile on gravel roads in heels had her cringing. But she really didn't want anyone to think she and Cache were dating. So she clutched her folder and put a smile on her face, each step toward the entrance of the ranch feeling like the journey of a lifetime.

Chapter Nine

"Why does she care?" Cache wondered to himself after he got Karla's text. So what if Scarlett knew they were going to dinner? Did it really matter?

He needed to find out. Tonight. He was going to find out tonight.

He also wanted to kiss Karla tonight, but he had a feeling it was too early for her. Heck, it was probably too early for him.

He pulled out of his driveway a few minutes before six, and he saw Karla mincing her way along the road. Sort of. It was the side of the road, in the grass, as her heels dangled from her fingers.

Cache pulled up alongside her and stopped so she could get in. "Thanks," she said, wiping her forehead. "I should've just had you come pick me up. Phew."

"Yeah," Cache said, going past Prime the welcoming

robot to the ranch. "Why didn't you?" He glanced at her. "What's the big secret?"

She lifted her shoulder in one sexy shrug. "I don't know. I'm just...sensitive to people talking about me."

Cache wanted to believe her, but something didn't feel quite right. "You sure that's all it is?"

"Yeah," she said. "I even told my sisters about you." She looked at him, twisting fully toward him. She wore a pair of black slacks with a purple blouse with flowing sleeves. She wore more makeup than Cache had seen on her face, and she was downright beautiful.

The truck started bumping unevenly, and Cache pulled it back onto the road as he put his eyes where they should be—on the road. He chuckled nervously, unsure of what they'd even been talking about.

"They're great," Karla said. "I sort of wish I could be there to help with the wedding prep."

"Oh, yeah?" Cache asked. "You like that kind of stuff?"

"I mean, yeah," Karla said. "It's frilly and fun, and I like dressing up as much as the next woman."

"You sure do look nice tonight," Cache said.

"Thank you."

"So tell me where we're going," he said, coming to the intersection down the bluff from the ranch.

"There's a great place down at the end of Market Street," Karla said, a new twinkle in her eye that really got Cache's blood humming through his system.

"They have food?" he asked.

"Yep," she said. "Turn right here."

He eased the truck off the dirt road in the direction she'd said, smiling despite himself. "What aren't you telling me?"

"This is an off-the-beaten-path type of place," she said.

"Expensive?" Cache asked, wishing he hadn't asked. He didn't know what he'd been thinking when he'd blurted out that he was broke. Thankfully, she hadn't asked him any questions, and Cache had been able to go home without explaining much more.

"They don't take money," Karla said.

"What?" Cache looked at her. "Is it a soup kitchen?"

"No," Karla said with a giggle. "It's a progressive diner. It's called Step It Up, and they don't take money."

Cache had no idea what she was talking about. "I don't understand most of what you just said," he finally said. "I mean, it was English, but I can't figure it out."

"You pay in steps," she said. "New customers get twenty thousand steps, so you'll be able to get something to eat."

"Pay in steps?" he repeated slowly, trying to make the words line up in his mind.

"Yeah," she said. "A cup of coffee is a thousand steps." She reached into her purse and pulled out a watch with a large face. "I've been tracking my steps all day, and I think I have enough for the ham and cheese omelet."

"Ah, breakfast for dinner," he said. "A woman after my

heart." They laughed together, and Cache wished she sat closer to him so he could hold her hand. Happiness pulled through him, and Cache hadn't realized how *not* happy he'd been these past few years.

And that wasn't even right. He wasn't unhappy. He struggled to identify what his life had been missing, but perhaps that was all it was. Something had been missing, and with Karla in the truck with him, that thing had been found.

Companionship. Friendship. A beautiful woman with him.

"What do you like?" she asked.

"Chicken fried steak and eggs," he said. "Do they have that?"

"I'm sure they do," she said.

"You don't like chicken fried steak?"

She shrugged again, and Cache really liked the movement in her shoulders. "I don't dislike it, but it's not my first choice."

"Will I have enough points for that?" he asked. "And how do they pay for their food?"

"They get grants from the city, state, and federal food programs," she said. "And there's a walking path that goes right behind it, so if you need more steps, you can get them easily."

"Wow," he said.

"So you better start wearing a watch or something to

track your steps," she said. "I bet you get a ton every day, and you can bank them up."

Cache felt a little light-headed. "This sounds kind of crazy," he said.

"It's fun," Karla said. "And it's right up there on the right."

Cache spotted it, the huge sneaker on top of the building hard to miss. He parked and got out, taking Karla's hand when they met at the front of the truck. "Let's go see what they have."

The vibe inside the diner was completely outside Cache's sphere. It was hip, and he was pretty much the opposite of that. But the menu was scrawled on the wall in chalk, and big, loopy letters spelled out that they did have chicken fried steak.

Karla stepped up to the counter, another wicked gleam in her eye. She first showed her phone and said, "Ham and cheese omelet," and went through choosing a biscuit over pancakes, and orange juice over coffee.

"And he's a new customer." She grinned at him.

Before Cache could even blink, a foghorn filled the restaurant, and he almost fell backward with the noise. "New customer," the girl there chirped, and every employee in the shop repeated it as if having a new customer they fed for free was the most amazing thing on the planet.

Every one of Cache's senses were overloaded, and

Karla ordered his chicken fried steak for him. "Pancakes?" the girl asked.

"Yes," Cache said.

"Oh, that's a mistake," Karla said, her lips barely moving. "The biscuit is the size of your head and *amazing*."

He looked from her to the girl taking the order. "Is that true?"

"The biscuits are delicious," she said.

"Fine, switch me to a biscuit," he said, and he chose orange juice instead of coffee as well. He got a card with less than five thousand steps left on it, and Karla's app got drained down to twelve steps for her omelet. They moved to a table in the corner, a shoe with the number twenty-four on it.

"This place is quirky," Cache said. "And I'm completely deaf from that horn."

"It's great, right?" Karla asked, peeling a wrapper off her straw.

"How did you find this place?" he asked.

"One of the volunteers at the ranch told me about it," she said. "Genevieve over in the Canine Club."

"Oh, right," he said, hoping he didn't have to say anything else about Genevieve. "Are you two friends?"

"I mean, friendly," she said. "Why?"

"No reason," he said, deciding to just tell her. "We went out once, and it was a complete disaster."

"Is that so?" Karla said, full flirt in her eyes.

"I'm hoping this won't turn out the same."

"I think it's going fine," Karla said, smiling.

"Me too," Cache said, smiling back. "So, Karla, what do you do for fun?"

"Oh, I don't know," she said, tucking her hair behind her ear. "I sure like watching my cowboy boyfriend play in his band."

THAT WEEKEND, Cache had double ranch chores because Dave was at Fort Irwin for his weekend Army training. He normally didn't mind, but this weekend, he'd really like to spend some time with Karla.

Instead, he worked the morning in the barn, medicating the horses, then over at the Canine Club as normal. He bypassed his cows for now and headed over to LlamaLand to take care of Dave's chores. He fed and watered, cleaned stalls, and moved over to Piggy Paradise, where he had more to do. Taking care of two men's jobs in one day was extremely difficult, but he liked the extra pay he got. Scarlett and Dave insisted he take the money for the weekend, and Cache had stopped arguing with them.

Sawyer came over to the fence where Cache worked, and he said, "I don't know how you ran this ranch alone."

"It wasn't easy," he said. "And it wasn't like this either. The ranch is at least ten times the operation it used to be."

"Yeah," Cache said. "How's the baby?"

A soft smile touched Sawyer's mouth. "Really great." He yawned. "I won't lie, though, I'm exhausted. I'm too old to be getting up in the middle of the night."

Cache chuckled with him and said, "Well, I have to go feed the chickens. See you at church tomorrow?"

"Yeah," Sawyer said, knocking on the fence post before he went on his way toward the stables.

By the time Cache made it to the cow pastures, twilight had gathered and all of his cows waited by the trough.

"Sorry, guys," he said, glancing down. But they'd already been watered. He glanced around as if the responsible party would be there, but he saw no one.

"Thank you," he whispered to the sky, as if God Himself had filled the troughs so Cache could stumble home to a hot shower and something to eat.

The scent of spicy Mexican food met his nose as he got out of his truck and headed toward his house. He was isolated now in his cabin, as his next-door neighbor on the right had been Hudson and he'd moved into the homestead when he and Scarlett had gotten married.

And around the U-shaped bend, Carson, Jeri, and Sawyer had all moved on. So Cache sat near the corner of the U-shaped Community all alone, with Lance on his right. He liked the cowboy perfectly fine, and he was the best drummer Cache had ever met. But he kept to himself almost all of the time, and he never had much to say, even during band practice.

But he was obviously eating well tonight. He sighed as he opened his front door and started to kick off his boots. He froze when he realized all the lights were on. Music played from somewhere. And the scent of Mexican food... that came from *his* kitchen.

Someone had clearly been here to set up this fiesta, but he couldn't see them. "Hello?" he called, thinking maybe someone had moved into his house while he'd been out working. Scarlett was hiring several new people, and his place was fairly stale. Maybe they'd thought this cabin was available.

Karla opened the back door and stepped inside, carrying a pair of oven mitts and a plate of something. "Oh, there you are," she said with a smile.

He finished kicking off his boots, his toes sighing in relief. "What are you doing here?" he asked.

"Making dinner," she said. "I know the Army weekends are rough."

Cache moved through the cabin and into the kitchen with her. "Wow, this is amazing. Thanks." He looked down at the bubbly pan of burritos. His eyes met Karla's, and everything else fell away.

Feeling reckless and bold, he reached up and cradled her face in one palm. "Is this keeping things secret?" he asked. "How many people saw you come over here?"

She grinned at him, full of playfulness and punch. "No one," she said. "I came really early today while everyone was still working."

"Smart," he said, enjoying this little game between them. "And I'm starving."

"Well, you've come to the right place to fix that," she said, opening a couple of cupboards before she found the plates. "And I won't even ask you how many steps you put in today."

Cache laughed, but by the way his feet ached, he had more than enough steps for anything on Karla's menu.

Chapter Ten

Karla laughed as she and Cache snuggled together on his couch. She hadn't anticipated quite how long she'd need to stay, but he said he didn't mind. They'd enjoyed the chile verde pork burritos she'd made, and he'd told her all about the dairy farm in Nevada where he'd grown up.

She sure liked listening to him talk, but when he'd put a movie on the small TV in the living room, that was fine too.

He'd fallen asleep the moment the movie had started, but Karla didn't mind. She liked the weight of his arm across her shoulder, enjoyed the deep, even way he breathed, and she craved the warmth of his body beside hers.

She giggled again at something on the movie, her

thoughts straying left and right as they'd been doing since he'd dozed off.

She wanted to admit she liked him. Wanted a relationship with him. One that wasn't hidden in the shadows because of her own insecurities. One she could shout to the world and answer questions about and feel confident in.

Why couldn't she do that?

"I like you," she whispered against his shirt, and he immediately shifted. Adrenaline spiked her heartbeat, but he didn't open his eyes and he didn't say anything. In fact, a soft snore rumbled through his throat, and somehow it was the sexiest thing Karla had ever heard.

The movie ended, and Karla delicately disentangled herself from his arms, waking him.

"I'm so sorry," he said groggily, wiping his hand down his face. "I slept through the whole thing, didn't I?"

"Yep." She grinned at him and slipped her shoes back on. "It's fine. You worked the job of two men today." She started to walk past him, but he took her hand in his, his fingers encircling her wrist.

She looked down at him, and time slowed to a stop. He was absolutely stunning without that cowboy hat on, though the sight of him wearing it also got her pulse accelerating. A smile crossed her face, though she hadn't expressly told her brain to do it.

"Look, I—" he started at the same time Karla leaned down and brushed her lips along his forehead.

Fear and foolishness hit her, and she tried to pull her hand away. Cache held it firmly now, refusing to let her go. He rose, crowding into her personal space. She stepped back, but he didn't let her go far.

"I was going to say I really appreciate you coming over and making me dinner." He gazed at her, the heated desire in those brilliant blue eyes scorching her.

"Yeah," she said stupidly. "I'm glad you liked the burritos."

Cache closed his head and dipped his head, but his aim was all off. He didn't kiss her—didn't even try. He wrapped both arms around her as if they were slow dancing and pressed his cheek to hers.

Comfort streamed through her, and she could get very used to having this man's presence in her life. "I like you without the hat," she murmured.

"Yeah?" he asked. "I feel a little naked without it."

She giggled, taking in a deep breath of his day-old cologne, his sweat, the crispness from something he used on his hair. "Do you sleep with it on, cowboy?"

"Sometimes," he admitted. "Especially if I'm catching a nap when I should be working."

She held onto his shoulders as they swayed, pure pleasure rolling through her. "I should go," she finally whispered.

"Yeah," he whispered back. "I'm real busy again tomorrow, but we're still on for church, right?"

The peace lessened, but Karla decided it was time to

figure out how she really felt about the Lord. Church. Religious things.

"Yes," she said, though part of her wished he'd be too busy to go.

"We don't have to go for long," Cache said. "I'll be sweaty from working, and I usually slip in late and leave early. But I like to go for a little bit."

"Text me when you're ready." Going late and leaving early sounded like a good plan for her, as she hadn't been to church in a while. "And how do you feel about mushrooms on pizza?"

"Everything belongs on pizza," he said, pulling back and smiling at her.

"All right, then," she said. "You stop by my cabin tomorrow night when you finish working, and I'll feed you again."

He leaned down again. "Thank you, Karla." The words whispered in her ear, and his lips caught on her earlobe for a microsecond. There, then gone. She froze, and he seemed to as well. Then he pressed his lips against her neck just below her ear, and a sigh moved through her whole body.

She wanted to taste him, but he never strayed toward her mouth. Instead, he lighted kisses down her neck to her shoulder and straightened. "You should definitely go," he said, his voice throaty and a wild look in his eyes.

Karla wasn't afraid of him, but she supposed their relationship was moving a little fast. So she tucked her hair, ducked her head, smiled, and headed for the front door. She twisted the knob, but Cache opened it fully, standing there with his hand higher up on the door while she slipped into the night.

The air was cooler out here than inside the cabin, and Karla took a deep breath as she hurried down his steps and out of the circle of light from his porch lamp. Once under the cover of darkness, she relaxed, every step back to her cabin filled with hope and the promise of a fun, loving relationship with Cache Bryant.

———

THE NEXT MORNING, Karla couldn't make herself get in the shower. The idea of going to church had been tolerable as she stood in Cache's arms the previous night. But now?

Now, she felt like throwing up.

She stood at the window in her bedroom, which looked out over the open land behind her cabin. At one point, she'd gone to Scarlett with an idea to make this wild area of the ranch into a tourist attraction. Cabins, a firepit, outdoor games, campsites, all of it. Jeri had even drawn up a few maps for the area, along with blueprints for different sized cabins.

But, in the end, the idea hadn't panned out. It would bring more money to the ranch, sure. But Forever Friends was worried about the impact tourists would have on the animal sanctuary, and everyone had decided that such an attraction wasn't necessary.

The ranch had plenty of money now that it had been up and in operation for a few years. Scarlett seemed to know what she was doing, as did everyone else who came to Last Chance Ranch to work.

Her phone sounded, and she glanced down at where it sat on the nightstand. *Ten minutes,* Cache had said.

And Karla still wore a pair of khaki shorts and a tank top with a yellow curry stain on it. She didn't move, though the moment teetered on important. If she was going to go to church with him, she'd better get ready.

Maybe she wouldn't go.

She picked up her phone and sent him a question. *Do you believe God forgives everything?*

Because Karla didn't. She'd gone too far down the wrong road. The Lord couldn't possibly love her. Not after what she'd done.

"And you'll have to tell Cache," she whispered to herself. She immediately rejected the idea of telling him she'd been unfaithful to her first husband. Even if Jackson was already cheating on her. Even if he'd already moved out. Karla had known it was wrong. They hadn't been divorced yet, and she shouldn't have gone out with anyone, much less spent any time with them in the bedroom.

She pressed against her stomach, as if the resulting life from that one-night stand was still inside her.

Cache's text came back with, *Yes. Luke 4. The woman at the well.*

Instant tears sprang to Karla's eyes. She knew the story of the woman at the well. A woman who lived in sin, and yet who the Savior ministered to. Taught.

Loved.

She turned away from the window, a tear running down her face. She wanted to feel comfortable thinking about the Lord. She wanted to feel like she belonged in church—and with Cache.

Right now, she didn't. But maybe if she went, she would.

Changing quickly, she pulled on a black skirt that swished nicely around her knees. She replaced the stained tank top with a bright blue blouse and had just pulled her heels on when Cache knocked on her back door.

No time for hair and makeup, she decided she could go to church with a fresh face and whatever her hair was currently doing. She ran her fingers through it as she went to answer the door, and she shared a few anxious seconds with Cache as they looked at one another.

"So you're coming?" he asked, his gaze sliding down her body and back to her face.

"Yes," she said. "I'm not one hundred percent put together. But you said you'd be going sweaty, so I figured I could go without earrings."

A smile formed on his mouth, and Karla couldn't look away from it. "You look great, sweetheart." He nodded toward his truck which idled on the gravel road behind her house. "Ready?"

"Yes."

He steadied her in her heels on the gravel and helped her into the truck. The ten minute drive to church felt like a death march, and Karla slicked her hands down her thighs when he pulled into a parking spot and turned off the vehicle.

"I don't know," she said, feeling that ball of emotion at the back of her throat again. "Cache, I—I've done some bad things."

He simply looked at her. "You don't have to be perfect to go to church."

"I know," she said, suddenly angry. "But you have to be good."

"Karla," he said, his voice somewhat reproving. He reached for her, but she kept her arms crossed against her stomach. If she moved, she was sure to be sick.

"What are we talking?" he asked. "Like, you've...well, I don't even know what to say. Have you been arrested? Sent to jail?"

"No," she said, tears coming again. Did she have to tell him? What if he walked away and never came back, the way Jackson had?

Number one, he's not Jackson, she told herself. *Number two, your marriage with Jackson had already been over by the time you'd told him about the cheating and the baby and the subsequent miscarriage.*

"Karla," he said again, the bell in the church starting to ring over the last syllable of her name.

She couldn't look at him. "You go in," she said. "I'll follow."

"Yeah, I don't think you will," he said. "You'll bolt as soon as I get out of this truck."

"I'm sorry," she said, feeling weak and so unlike herself. This new person she'd become at Last Chance Ranch didn't feel like this. Didn't have to. "This is why I don't date."

"Why is that again?" Cache asked, seemingly nonplussed about the bell and the few people hurrying inside the gray building with the cross on top.

Karla just needed to blurt it out. Short sentences. Like ripping off a bandage.

But this bandage had been fused to her heart for five years, and she knew yanking on it would probably cause too much bleeding.

She said, "I cheated on my husband and got pregnant," anyway. She didn't want to look at Cache, but her eyes seemed to do whatever they wanted despite her protests.

He blinked, shocked and disgusted with her.

She reached for the door handle, ready to bolt right now.

Chapter Eleven

C ache was still absorbing what Karla had said when she flew from the truck. "Hey," he said after her, slow on the uptake. When she'd said she hadn't been to jail, Cache had relaxed. How bad could it be if she hadn't killed someone?

But cheating was pretty bad.

He launched himself out of the truck to follow her. Dang, the woman could move fast in heels, and she'd already crossed the parking lot to the walking path that ran behind the church and circled the bluff where the ranch sat.

He didn't want to yell after her. Or run, both of which would've called attention to them. And Karla had been quite clear she didn't want any attention on her, or their relationship.

He finally caught her several paces behind the church,

thinking he should get double the steps for panicked speed-walking at Step It Up. Not that he'd bought a smart watch or any device to track his steps since their date on Monday night.

Karla wasn't wearing hers today either.

He just walked beside her, at a complete loss as to what to say. He tried praying, but his thoughts felt all blocked up. When the fury finally faded from her steps, he asked, "So you have a child?"

"No," she bit out.

Cache waited for more, but she didn't seem to be in a talkative mood anymore. "Karla," he said, a hint of frustration in her name. "Can you just stop for a second?" He touched her arm, and she flinched away from him but stopped walking.

He moved in front of her so he could see her face. "Yes, I think God forgives infidelity. I do." He drew in a big breath, feeling stronger with the words—the knowledge he possessed about God. "He can forgive you for this."

She shook her head. "I don't know, Cache."

"Then you just have to find out for yourself," he said gently. Despite what he'd just learned, he wanted to be with her still. Her soul called to his in such a strong way, and he couldn't ignore that any longer.

He reached toward her slowly, giving her every opportunity to fall back, put more distance between them. She didn't, and he finally took both of her hands in his. "Look," he said softly, his voice barely louder than the breeze. "Maybe you just need to borrow my faith for a while until you find yours again."

Because he believed she still had it. Her faith had just gone cold, dormant. But it was still there.

"I feel...dirty," she said, her voice breaking on the last word. Cache enveloped her in his arms, wishing he could take her pain, her anguish, her sorrow. He couldn't, but he knew who could.

"Let's just sit in the back for ten minutes," he whispered into her hair. "Okay? Just see how you feel." He didn't want to push her. Heaven knew he didn't like being forced into anything.

Please help her, he prayed, finally centering his thoughts on the most important thing. Karla. Not what she'd done. Those were just actions. *She* was a person— and a good one.

"You're a good person," he said next. "You belong here, even if you don't feel like it yet."

She nodded against his shoulder, and he tucked one arm against his side and headed back to the church.

By the time they slipped in the back, the sermon was more than half over. It didn't matter that Cache didn't know what the pastor was talking about. It didn't matter that they'd missed his favorite part of the meeting—the musical numbers.

It only mattered that he was there, able to bask in the life-giving light of the Lord.

He could only hope and pray Karla felt it too.

She didn't run, and she didn't cry, so Cache considered both of those wins. She sat ramrod straight next to him, her nerves pouring off of her in waves, but she stayed. She seemed to be listening, her eyes glued to Pastor Williams at the front of the chapel.

A few minutes later, a mother with a crying baby got up to leave. Cache nudged Karla, and she got up without hesitation and practically sprinted out the nearby door, almost trampling the mother in her haste.

Cache followed her and found her outside in the shade of the huge tree beside the church, doubled over with her hands braced on her knees. At least she was still breathing.

"Come on," he said kindly. "Let's get out of here." He mourned the loss of his safe, tranquil time at church. But he told himself there'd be another opportunity next week, and Karla needed him more than he needed to be in that chapel.

He didn't turn back toward the ranch, but instead started toward town. She didn't seem to notice for a few minutes, and then she swung her attention toward him. "Where are we going?"

"We need food," he said. "And pie. I feel like pie. Don't you?" He pulled into a diner he'd frequented several times. It wasn't as busy as The Finer Diner, and they didn't have live music.

But they had great pie in a variety of flavors.

"Cache," she said. "I just want to go home."

"Well, we don't always get what we want." He grinned at her and got out of the truck. She stayed stubbornly inside until he'd walked around the whole vehicle and opened her door for her. "Sweetheart, they have peach pie here that will blow your mind. Come on. Please." He hated begging, but he couldn't just take her back to her cabin and let her retreat from him.

"Peach pie?"

"The best on the planet," he said. "Better than yours."

That got her out of the truck, and Cache smiled again when she put her hand in his first. "You're not...you don't have a million questions for me?" she asked as they crossed the hot parking lot and went inside the diner.

He waited to answer until they had a table with ice water sitting in front of them. "I suppose I do," he said. "But they're not important right now. How did you feel at church?"

"Scared," she admitted, some of that fear running through her eyes right now. "But it was...okay."

"So next week, we go for twenty minutes," he said, watching her. Like closing blinds, she drew a wall over her expression. So maybe not.

He lifted his water to his lips and sipped. Could he go to church for the rest of his life by himself? He'd known Karla hadn't been to church, but he'd never suspected why.

"I lost the baby at ten weeks," she said out of nowhere,

and Cache worked hard to school his own expression. Draw those same shutters over it so she couldn't see his immediate reaction.

"I'm sorry," he said. "That must've—was that hard?" He didn't want to assume he knew what she'd gone through. He didn't. Couldn't even fathom it.

She shook her head, her hair falling over her shoulders and hiding some of her face. "It was hard, but the real reason I'm such a horrible person is because I was...happy about it." She covered her face with both hands, and Cache shook his head at the approaching waitress.

She looked horrified, and Cache understood how things seemed at his table. He held up a couple of fingers and focused on Karla again. Without thinking too hard about anything, he slipped over to the other side of the table and wrapped one arm around her.

"Shh," he whispered. "It's okay. You're okay."

THAT EVENING, after all the chores were finally done, Cache stood in the gathering darkness, his soul open before the Lord. He'd been thinking about Karla non-stop since that morning, and everything felt like a muddy mess.

"I like this woman," he said to the first twinklings of the stars. "Do I give up on her because she's made some mistakes?"

That felt absolutely wrong. He'd made mistakes in his

life too. Maybe not as big as hers. Maybe not as emotionally scarring. Maybe not as long-lasting. But mistakes nonetheless.

He'd been asking himself since she'd quieted enough to eat her peach pie and ice cream if *he* could forgive her, which sounded stupid. She hadn't cheated on him. But the thought was that she *could*, and Cache didn't like that it was there, poisoning his mind.

"What should I do?" he asked next, and he immediately thought he should join Karla for dinner, as they'd planned.

At least that had been the plan last night.

He washed his hands in ice cold water from the pump near the pigpens and headed down the gravel road. He felt alone, though there were dozens of people who lived on this ranch. He had friends he trusted and family he could call.

But he'd never felt so alone.

He knocked on Karla's door, the light within giving off the air of cheeriness. She didn't answer, and he knocked again.

When she still didn't come to the door, he sat on her top step and pulled out his phone. *I just want to see you,* he typed out. *Make sure you're okay.*

He didn't care about the food, though his stomach was eating itself inside out. Was he bothering her? Inserting himself in her life when she didn't want him?

He sent the text anyway, a severe kind of desperation

working its way up his throat. If she didn't answer this time, fine. He'd go home and order pizza, keep his head down, and—yeah, there was no *and*.

Cache wanted Karla Jenkins, plain and simple. He wanted to know everything about her, the good, the bad, the ugly. He wanted her presence in his life. He wanted to help her, and have her help him.

He got up to knock again, but as he turned toward the door, it opened. Karla stood there, her beautiful blonde hair in strings around her face. She was already crying.

Cache rushed toward her and gathered her close, pressing her back into the privacy of her cabin. "Hey, I'm here now," he whispered. "I'm here, and everything is going to be fine."

"You're too good for me," she whispered.

Cache wiped her tears and shook his head. "Nope. Not true."

"Aren't you worried I'll cheat on you too?"

"Nope," he said just as quickly. "I'm not."

"Why not?"

"Because, Karla, if we do this, if we're really together, and in love, and married, and...." His voice stuck on all he'd said. He was talking way too far down the road, but Karla just gazed up at him, waiting for him to finish.

"I trust you," he finally said. "And I trust God, and I think we'd be great together. So no, I'm not worried about you cheating on me, because I believe our relationship could be exactly what we both want."

He looked at her, almost desperate for her to say something back to him. Something to let him know that she felt the same way about him.

Something.

Anything.

Chapter Twelve

Karla saw the anxiety in Cache's eyes. She wanted to erase it, but she'd blown open their entire relationship. Their friendship too.

Bombed it.

He was too good for her, despite his protests.

"I made pizza," she said, stepping out of his arms in an attempt to make the moment less awkward. "I know you like all the meats, and...." She trailed off as she went into the kitchen but he stayed by the back door. "You don't want to eat."

"I want to know how you feel about me," he said, his voice on the low end of dangerous. "I basically just poured my heart out to you, and you started talking about pizza."

Karla blinked at him, surprised. He was so calm all the time. So witty. So light-hearted. "Food is how I show I care about a person," she said. "I didn't realize I needed to say it out loud."

The anger slid right off his face. "Really?"

"Cache, I went to your place yesterday and cooked for you for three hours. I wouldn't have done that if I wasn't madly crushing on you." She turned away, embarrassed by the words. She wasn't great at saying how she felt. The food should convey that message.

Cache joined her in the kitchen, his body heat next to hers as soothing as the scent of marinara still hanging in the air.

"I made the sauce from scratch," she said, wishing her voice didn't sound so strangled. "It took all afternoon." She looked up at him, fireworks popping when their eyes met.

"I think you're beautiful," he said, tucking an errant piece of hair behind her ear. Of course, they were all errant, as she'd done nothing with her hair that day and hadn't showered in two.

"I put on all the meats, because I know you like them. And olives, and green peppers, and mushrooms." She indicated the cheesy pizza that had come out of the oven ten minutes ago. She hadn't been sure Cache would still show, but she was so, so happy he had.

Cache grinned at her, and the mood lightened considerably. "You're an amazing woman, Karla." He touched his lips to her temple and said, "And I'm *starving*."

Karla busied herself with making punch and getting

down plates. He held her hand and bent his head to say a prayer.

"And please bless Karla that she'll know how much she's loved," he said, causing her breath to hitch in her throat. She didn't hear another word of his prayer, but she managed to squeeze, "Amen," out of her mouth after he'd said it.

"I never did ask you what you thought of the peach pie," he said, sitting down at her small dining room table like he'd eaten there plenty of times in the past. He hadn't, but she sure did like the sight of him there.

"It was delicious," she said. "But I don't see how you think it's better than mine."

"They put something in it," he said. "Nutmeg or cinnamon...something. I can't put my finger on it." He bit into a slice of pizza, and his eyes rolled back in his head as he moaned.

"Karla," he said around the mouthful of food, and she laughed.

He swallowed and said, "Sweetheart, I sure am glad you know how to cook."

She was too, as it brought her a lot of joy to feed those she cared about. And she did care about Cache. A lot.

Eating dinner beside him felt fabulous, and by the time he stepped out her back door, she was starting to feel more like herself again. Her new self. The woman she'd become since leaving behind her life in the city.

A tiny ray of hope entered her heart, and she pressed her eyes closed, whispering, "Thank you," and hoping God wasn't too mad at her that He wouldn't hear.

THE NEXT DAY, Karla went to the cuddling cows and rinsed out their water trough. They snacked on grass all day long, but even she knew animals needed fresh, cold water. Especially in the summer heat, now that June had arrived.

Cache would be by in a little bit, after he finished his work at the Canine Club. Karla rinsed and sprayed off the loose grass that had stuck to the metal trough, finally setting the hose in it to fill.

None of the cows approached her the way they did Cache, but that was all right. She'd practiced with them a little bit on Saturday afternoon when she'd stopped by to fill the troughs, and she could get a couple of them to lay down and let her cuddle with them.

She still didn't know their names, because all cows looked identical to her. One turned toward her, a low moo coming from her mouth. "Hey, girl," Karla said. "Down."

The cow seemed to give her a very bovinial glare, but down she went. Karla had no treat, and the last time she'd tried to act like these cows were dogs, she'd hit one of them with an apple.

"Good girl," she said anyway, holding out her palm. "Stay." She gave the cow a few seconds to obey, and then she stepped over her front legs and cuddled into the warmth of the cow's body. "Ah, that's nice," she said, gazing up at the blue, blue sky. So blue it seemed impossible something should be that color.

"What can you tell me about your owner?" she asked. "Is he really that kind? That good?"

Sure, she'd seen the turmoil on his face in the truck, but he hadn't asked her a million questions, and she hadn't felt judged.

She hadn't wanted anyone to know her secrets. Her last secret relationship had torn a hole right through her soul, and she didn't want to go through that again.

Of course, everything about this secret relationship was different. For starters, she wasn't married. Secondly, Cache wasn't some guy she'd met at a party. Third, *she* was different.

"I'm different," she said to the sky, a measure of peace filling her. "I'm sorry," she whispered next. "I want to do better. I do."

Sitting in church had been an exquisite form of torture. Surely the pastor would be able to feel the sin radiating off of her, but he'd simply continued on with his sermon. In the short time she'd been in the chapel, she'd heard him say that the Lord was mindful of all of his children.

And funnily enough, Karla had believed him.

Still, it was much easier to breathe outside the church than in, and she couldn't believe how kind Cache had been after her confessions. Of course they mattered, but they hadn't driven him away.

She sighed into the cow, happier today than she'd been yesterday. Then, when the time grew close to when Cache would show up, she slipped away from the dairy cow and headed back to her cabin.

After all, she had a brand new cow cuddling website to build, and that was going to take most of the day.

TIME MARCHED FORWARD, and the first couple of weeks of June slipped through her fingers like smoke. Cache continued to stop by and see her after dark. Sometimes she snuck into his place while the cowboys were still working.

She had meetings with Scarlett and Adele, learned that her next-door neighbor was pregnant, and put the appropriate amount of effort and happiness into her job, her friendships, and feeding the cowboys on the ranch.

Her life felt fuller now than it ever had before, and she knew the reason. Cache Bryant.

She'd never told him she was the one showing up in his pasture to water his cows. He never told her someone was doing that for him. Karla relished that secret too.

She did attend church with him two more times,

adding ten minutes to each session. It wasn't horrible, and she'd felt a tiny flicker of faith start to grow in her chest. Cache seemed to have all the faith in the world, but she pushed against the negative thoughts that she needed to be like him.

That was impossible anyway. The man could lift a hundred pounds right over his head.

Karla smiled at her own wit and finished designing a flyer for the Fourth of July picnic partnership happening in a few weeks. Surprisingly enough, Forever Friends, Last Chance Ranch, and the church were putting on a three-tiered event.

Dog adoptions, dinner, and fireworks. Karla had been working for weeks to get the word out to the community, and she'd be going on a local morning show next week to talk about the event.

She'd spent some time in the fields with Cache, too, and they could get six cows in a circular formation now. She'd never cuddled with him, each of them choosing their own cows to work with throughout the session. But they'd spent plenty of time in the evenings eating, talking, and snuggling together.

He still hadn't kissed her, and Karla wondered what he was waiting for. Every time she thought about it, her mind wove right over to the dark side, yelling things about her unworthiness and inability to be forgiven for the ugly things in her past.

But Cache didn't treat her like that. Scarlett praised

her for everything she did, and slowly, Karla was silencing the voices.

Oh, so slowly.

At least that was what she told Morning Glory as she cuddled into her one morning. They'd talked a lot about Cache too, but Glory didn't seem to have any strong opinions about the cowboy the way Karla did.

The sound of the gate swinging closed had her startling, and she realized she'd been cuddling with the cow too long.

Cache had arrived from the Canine Club.

"Glory," he called, but the cow didn't move.

"Good girl," Karla said softly, patting her side. She knelt up and looked over the cow to find him several paces away.

His steps stuttered, and then he tipped his head toward the sky and laughed. And laughed.

Karla couldn't help smiling, but she had no idea what was so dang funny. He was still chuckling as he came around Morning Glory and stepped into the space where she still was.

"Room for one more?" he asked.

Karla shifted toward Glory's front legs. "Maybe if your shoulders weren't as wide as a barge."

He nudged her with one of those shoulders deliberately, a mischievous twinkle in his eye. "You're the one who's been watering my cows."

"Yeah, well, I know how busy you are."

He laced his fingers through hers. "And you're cuddling with them and sneaking away before I get here." He wore questions in his expression now, and Karla didn't know how to answer them.

"We work together with the cows," she said.

"Mm hmm," he said, a clear prompt for her to keep talking.

"And I like...I like talking to them. Well, just Glory really. She keeps a lot of secrets for me."

"I'll bet she does." His hand on hers tightened. "What do you tell them?"

"If I told you, they wouldn't be secrets."

"Nope."

"It's good stuff," she said, sinking into his side though the day was already warm, and she didn't need the extra body heat. "Mostly about you. Glory won't tell me a dang thing."

He chuckled again, sweeping his lips across her cheek.

"And I don't know," she said. "It's nice here. It feels like I've stepped out of my real life into this small space." She shrugged. "In here, things make sense."

"Hmm." The humming vibrated his body and skipped over to hers too. "How are things going with the flyers?"

"Great," she said. "Almost done. Then I'm back to the website."

"Think we'll be ready by July Fourth?"

"Yep," she said, bound and determined to have information about the ranch's adoptions—and not just cats and dogs like most people thought—goat yoga, *and* cow cuddling ready for the community event at the church.

"So I have a confession," Cache said, glancing at Karla in a way that made her heart send out three beats in one. "Do you want to hear it?"

Chapter Thirteen

"I s that a real question?" Karla asked. "Of course I want to hear it."

Cache hadn't told a single soul what he'd considered telling Karla. He hesitated, deciding against saying anything more about his finances. He'd been oscillating about it for a couple of weeks now, since she'd told him about her previous relationships, her baby, and her insecurities.

They'd grown closer as they worked together, saw each other, and interacted over the past few weeks. Cache knew that was because he understood her better. Knew what made her tick.

"Are you going to tell me?" she asked.

"Yeah," he said. "I'm just trying to figure out what to say."

"It's better if you just rip it off," she said. "Like a bandage. Blurt it out."

Cache opened his mouth to do just that, and said, "I'm broke because of a previous gambling problem."

He drew in a breath as if he hadn't been doing so since arriving in the pasture. The space between him and Karla was intimate, only a few inches.

Her eyes searched his, compassion and concern there. "Do you still have that problem?"

"No," he said. "I mean, sometimes I think about it, obviously. The way you think about...things from your past." He shook his head and looked at his calloused hands. "But no."

She let several seconds of silence go by. "How much debt?"

"Twenty thousand," he said, his voice dropping to a whisper. But he wasn't ashamed. He'd made things right between him and the Lord, and now he just had to deal with the temporal consequences of his prior behavior.

"I'm okay," he said. "I just wanted you to know."

She squeezed his hand. "You're a good man, Cache."

"You think so? After knowing that I've done some bad things too?"

"Yeah, of course."

"That's so interesting," he said.

"It is? Why?"

Could she really not see it? He looked at her, the sun overhead starting to beat down on him a little too hotly. Or maybe his blood started pumping extra hard because of the glint of desire he saw in her eyes, or the way her gaze dropped to his mouth and rebounded back to his.

"Because if I'm a good person after doing some bad things, don't you think you are too?"

"I—" She clamped her mouth shut and looked away. "I'm working on it," she said.

"I know you are," he said, leaning over and pressing a kiss to her cheek. "And you're doing great. I mean, we went to church for thirty minutes last time. That's about half."

A smile touched her lips for only a moment. There, then gone. "I like taking care of the cows for you," she said softly.

"You do a lot for me," he said. "I've never eaten so great, or actually...." He paused, not quite sure she was ready for this confession.

"What?" she asked, looking at him.

"I know you show how you feel by what you do," he said. "I'm more of a sayer. And Karla, I've never been happier than I've been the last few weeks with you."

Everything in her face softened, and Cache allowed himself to look at her mouth now. It was perfectly kissable, her lips oh-so-inviting.

He leaned toward her, hoping she'd make a move too. Her eyelids drifted closed, and Cache took that as a sign that he had her permission to kiss her.

His hand on hers tightened as he drew closer. His own

eyes closed. And then his lips touched hers. He detected a trembling there, and he pressed harder, kissing her like he'd been dreaming of doing for so long.

She kissed him back, and before long, he felt her fingers on his face, pushing his hat off, and curling around his ears.

His desire to show her how he felt surged forward, and right there as they cuddled with Morning Glory, he kissed her and kissed her and kissed her.

He finally got control of himself and pulled away. "Wow," he whispered, opening his eyes to look at her. He'd mussed up her hair by running his hands through it, but she was still absolutely gorgeous.

Karla giggled as their eyes met, and she dropped her gaze to her lap. "Yeah," she said, snuggling into his side, her face pressed against his chest and both of her hands covering one of his. "Wow."

"THAT NOTE IS NOT RIGHT," Sawyer said over the drums. Since he stood so close to Cache, he could hear him and stopped playing. Dave quit too, and everyone looked at Sawyer.

"Fix it then," Cache said, feeling frustrated with the band. No one seemed to care about performing the way he did. Dave, especially, as he continued to date Sissy. He knew things were sort of stalled with them, but he didn't know how to help. And they really did need to practice.

Sawyer picked up a pencil and started scratching something out on the paper in front of him. He plucked strings from time to time, frowning and making changes. Dave set his guitar aside and went into Cache's kitchen for something to drink.

Lance actually provided all of the beverages, something Cache was very grateful for. He'd offered to pay Lance back, but the man had refused. He stepped over to the drum set that was a permanent fixture in his living room and tried not to roll his eyes.

"Just give him his time," Lance said under his breath.

"I know," Cache said. "Do you think we should try for another gig in July?"

"I think if you do, you'll make a gasket in Dave's head blow."

Cache laughed with Lance.

"Where have you been disappearing to at night?" Lance asked, picking up his can of soda.

"Nowhere," Cache said. He'd believed Karla when she said she just didn't want people talking about her. She had some secrets and had probably imagined that everyone knew what they were.

Cache understood that on a much deeper level than he wanted to.

"I don't believe you," Lance said. "Sometimes there are lights on here when I know you're not here, and there's been some mighty delicious smells coming from your house, and you don't cook."

Cache glanced over his shoulder to the kitchen, where Dave stood at the back door. Sawyer was still busy with the sheet music, seemingly in his own world.

"Fine," he whispered. "But you can't tell anyone."

"Who would I tell?" Lance asked. "You're my best friend."

"I'm seeing Karla Jenkins," Cache said. "It's not common knowledge, and I'll deny it to the death if you say something."

Lance's eyes widened. "Wow, Cache." He grinned at him. "Good for you."

"Yeah." Cache couldn't help smiling too. "So what about you? Any progress with Amber?"

"Am I interested in Amber?" Lance asked, glancing away.

"Well, you volunteer every Tuesday," Cache said. "I didn't realize it was because you have a heart of gold."

"Yeah, well, maybe I do." Lance looked at him and smiled, and Cache shook his head.

"All right."

"Ready," Sawyer said, passing out the pages with the new music on it. Dave returned to the living room, picked up his guitar, and they played.

Cache loved the freedom that came with the simple action of playing the guitar. Singing some backup vocals. Feeling like he was part of something bigger than him.

In fact, that feeling was what had rescued him from the edge of a complete breakdown. Last time he'd needed something like this, it had come in the form of his family. Leo and his father coming into Cache's bedroom at the house on the dairy farm and intervening in Cache's gambling habit.

That felt so long ago, and yet it had only been four years.

Cache definitely knew there were some things a man had to spend his whole life paying for.

Their practice broke up after that, and Dave seemed happier than he had when practice started. He lingered after the others left—especially Sawyer, who sure could take his sweet time on the music but bolted the moment he could.

Cache supposed he did have a wife and a new baby now, and he was glad Sawyer hadn't quit the band entirely. He wondered if Karla wanted kids at all, or if she'd just been relieved her last pregnancy had failed because of how it began.

"How's the base?" Cache asked.

"Great." Dave looked tired, and Cache knew he'd been taking on a lot out at the pet cemetery this summer. "What's going on with you?"

"Not much," Cache said, wishing he had some of Karla's pizza. In fact, he could probably go over to her house and find some.... The thought danced around in his head, making him smile when he shouldn't have.

And Dave saw it.

"Yeah, I think something's going on," he said.

Cache had already confessed about the secret relationship to one person. If Dave knew, then Sissy would find out, and before Cache knew it, everyone on the ranch would be talking about them.

Exactly what Karla didn't want.

"Really," Cache said. "Nothing."

"You've been comin' over to Horse Heaven later than usual." Dave folded his arms as if he could intimidate Cache by making himself look bigger. Well, Cache could fold his arms too, thank you very much, and he was no lightweight.

"Yeah," he said, setting his guitar in the corner near the front door. He turned and started picking up soda cans and water bottles. "I'm...dealing with the cows in between chores."

Dave accepted that, nodded, and picked up a couple of cans too. "You and those cows."

"Yeah," he said. If only he could tell Dave all about the cow cuddling, but things weren't quite ready yet, and Scarlett hadn't given the go-ahead. The cows were ready. Karla was working on the website. They had preliminary plans to have everything ready for the Fourth of July shindig down at the church.

A tremor of nerves ran through Cache. What if no one signed up? What if Scarlett wanted to keep all of the money from the cow cuddling?

Cache needed to talk to her, and he determined to do that tomorrow morning.

"Why are you hanging around here?" Cache asked. "Don't you have a girlfriend you can go kiss?"

Dave laughed, the sound truly joyous. Cache grinned at him, but it was time for Dave to go, and Cache practically shoved him out the front door.

He felt like a caged tiger as he forced himself to wait ten minutes. He turned off all the lights in the cabin except for the one above the kitchen sink. Nothing abnormal about that; it wasn't even nine o'clock yet, and Cache worked hard. Lance wouldn't be able to make assumptions about Cache and Karla—unless of course, he saw Cache sneak out his back door and cross through his backyard on his way to her cabin.

He really needed a couple of pieces of pizza—and to kiss the woman who made them.

Chapter Fourteen

Karla woke the next morning, trying to remember what day it was. She yawned, her eyes drier than normal, and wished she could go back to sleep. She stayed in bed, but falling back asleep was fruitless. Once she was awake, she couldn't go back to sleep.

The exhaustion level of entertaining Cache late at night was more than she'd anticipated. Probably because she was no spring chicken anymore. Semi-frustrated at herself for such a lame idiom, even inside her own mind, she got up and raked her fingers through her hair.

She didn't always work on ranch business on the weekends. Scarlett didn't expect her to, because if Karla lived down in Pasadena the way Amber and Sissy did, she'd have neighbors and friends outside of the ranch. She'd be able to go walking on Saturday morning or take her dog to the park. Go to lunch with her girlfriends.

Living on the ranch had been interesting, and it had taken her several months to carve out a routine that didn't have her working seven days a week.

Sitting on the edge of her bed, Karla took a moment to say a prayer. Her journey back to the Lord was going to take a while, and she knew that. Felt it way down deep in her soul. She was just glad she could feel her soul again.

"Thank you for a great night with Cache. Bless me with a relaxing weekend." She hadn't known one of those for a while—especially since going back to church brought her so much anxiety—but she felt good about today.

The website was done and ready to start accepting registrations. If anyone found it by clicking around, they could sign up. A hint of trepidation clicked through her, because if people signed up, then cow cuddling became real.

For some reason, she liked that it was something only she and Cache knew about right now. Sure, others on the ranch knew about it intellectually. But Karla liked that she and Cache had such intimate experience with it.

She brewed coffee and sat in front of the computer to finish a few final details for the posters and flyers for the Fourth of July events in a couple of weeks.

About mid-morning, someone knocked on her front door. She glanced toward it, her neck stiff from staring at the screen for so long. Cache always came to the back door, so as Karla got up and went to the door, she expected to see Scarlett standing there.

But it was Cache. "Oh," she said, glancing at the little of the backyard of the homestead she could see past his body. "What are you doing here?" She didn't mean for her voice to come out quite so hiss-like.

"Scarlett approved my request." He grinned like he'd won the lottery—and that would be a very big victory for Cache. If he gambled like that, which he didn't.

"That's great," she said.

He laughed, the carefree, laid-back cowboy she'd first met on the ranch returning. Karla sure did like his appearance, though she enjoyed Cache's more serious side too. His kind side. His caring side. The side that held her and promised her everything would be fine, because he was there.

Oh, yeah. There was a lot to like about Cache Bryant.

"So let's go over it," he said, coming into her cabin. She loitered in the doorway, checking the yard. No one was there, but that didn't mean people hadn't seen him standing on the front porch.

Who cares? she asked herself. She was allowed to date Cache. But for some reason, she wanted to keep their relationship a secret a little longer. Just until she was ready to have the spotlight on her.

She backed up, closed the door, and turned to find him inches behind her, that desire-filled glint in his eyes. He kissed her, pushing her against the door she'd just closed.

"I missed you," he murmured against her lips before claiming them again. Karla felt herself falling for him, and she desperately tried to hold on as he deepened the kiss.

Heat filled her, and her face felt flushed when he finally pulled away. "Okay," she said, breathing in the masculine scent of his skin, the woodsy quality of his cologne, the glorious weight of his hand on her hip.

"So you're happy about the approval."

"Yeah," he whispered, this serious version of Cache also sexy and a man to be admired. "And it's better than I thought." He backed up a couple of steps, finally turning and walking over to her couch. He sank onto it with a sigh and held out the folder in his hand.

Karla took it from him and perched on the edge of the loveseat beside him. She grinned at him before flipping open the folder to look inside. She scanned, reading quickly, and finally looking up at him as wonder spread through her.

"Cache," she said. "She approved eighty percent?"

"They're my cows," he said simply.

"And you've done all the work."

"Well, not all of it," he said, smiling again. He leaned his head back and closed his eyes. "It's almost fourteen hundred dollars per session."

Karla did the math quickly, using her phone as a calculator. "Actually, if we get six couples per session, and you get eighty percent of the fee, it's just *over* fourteen hundred dollars per session."

She tilted her phone toward him so he could see the

1440 on the screen. But he had his eyes closed, and he looked absolutely gorgeous as he sat there with a look of pure peace and contentment on his face.

And Karla knew in that moment that the Lord had answered her prayers. His too, probably, but definitely hers. Because this was going to be a great weekend.

THE DAYS MARCHED ON, and June started to die. Karla spent time with Cache every day in the cow pastures and usually at night too.

The last Sunday of the month, she and Cache stayed for the entire sermon at church, and Karla felt a new, invigorating sense of life come over her. As she sat there, listening to Pastor Williams talk about letting her light shine before the world, Karla finally felt like she *had* a light again.

She made lunch a few times a week for the people on the ranch, in addition to her marketing duties. She'd announced the cow cuddling during the morning show she'd been on at the end of last week, and they had five sessions full already.

Five.

Almost three full weeks, as she and Cache had decided to do two sessions per week. One on Saturday mornings, which had filled up first. And one on Wednesday evenings. That way, Cache wouldn't be stressed about getting his chores done, and the cows would have plenty of time to improve their cuddling techniques should they need extra training in between sessions.

Soup and salad bar for lunch today, she sent to everyone on the ranch. She stepped over to the stove and stirred the chicken noodle. She felt a little insane for making soup in the middle of the summer, but she decided she didn't care.

Number one, she *was* a little insane. Number two, her sausage tortellini soup was to die for. She smiled, hummed to herself, and got everything set up on the lawn outside her cabin.

Cache came by to help her set up the tents, and she couldn't help glancing at him every so often. Their eyes met, and that electric charge zipped through them. "You coming to lunch later?" she asked as she put a folding chair at the table where he'd just put one.

He glanced left, then right, then behind him. "Yep." He leaned down and kissed her. Something quick and light, but a kiss that zapped her pulse into an irregular beat.

She ducked her head and smiled as he finished with the chairs, waved to her, and left. He'd be back—but so would everyone else.

Eleven-thirty came, and Karla started serving soup to the first few cowboys that showed up. She'd feed anyone who came through the line, and sometimes volunteers joined the cowboys. Not many, but a few.

Karla enjoyed the sound of people talking. The laughter. Even the dull roar of the fan that tried to keep the mid-summer California heat from being too unbearable.

Cache came through the line and asked for the tortellini soup. "Seen Sissy yet?" he asked.

"No," Karla said, her eyes automatically moving to the corner of the homestead. "She'll come. She's just a little later than most." They needed to talk to the ranch accountant today about the cow cuddling. Scarlett had approved Cache's request for how much he'd get paid, but they needed accounts set up and a way to get paid by the ranch too.

And for that, they needed Sissy Longston.

More people went through the line, and Karla started to get nervous at Sissy's absence—especially when Dave showed up without her. Those two had been joined at the hip—or the lips—for several weeks now.

She was just about to pull out her phone and specifically text Sissy when the woman appeared at the corner of the house. She paused and scanned the scene before her, and even from a distance Karla could see the fury on her face.

Oh, so she and Dave weren't getting along.

A pinch of sadness hit Karla, and she ducked her head to check on the salad bowl. It was fine, of course.

Sissy arrived at the table—a miracle in Karla's opinion, what with the heels she wore. How she walked on grass in those was a mystery. "Hey, Karla," she said loudly. "This looks so good."

"You've got a couple of choices," Karla said, wishing she could reassure Sissy the way Cache did for her. "This is sausage tortellini soup. Or the regular chicken noodle." She looked at Sissy for her choice, trying to convey that she cared about her.

"Sausage tortellini."

Karla ladled soup into Sissy's bowl. She moved down to build her salad, and when she had her food ready, she turned back to the tables, clearly hesitating. Genevieve and Ames arrived, and Karla distracted herself by serving them.

She wouldn't want someone to ask her what was wrong if she was having a tough time with her boyfriend. In fact, she'd *hated* it when her friends back in the city had asked about Jackson. About the divorce. How she was doing.

How did they think she was doing?

No, Karla didn't need any spotlights on her, and neither did Sissy.

A moment later, she moved over to the table where Cache had his folder of cow cuddling information spread before Amber and Adele.

Karla hurried to finish serving, and she left the ladles in the bowls so people could serve themselves. It was almost two o'clock, and lunch would be over in a few minutes anyway.

"You tell her Cache." Adele beamed at the cowboy as Karla arrived and sat beside him. She almost put her hand on his leg under the table but stopped herself just in time.

He glanced at her and then back to Sissy, his face turning a bit red. He cleared his throat. "I've been working with my cows," he started. "And Adele trained all the goats for the yoga program."

"Amber trains them now," Adele said.

"Yeah, I know," Cache said. "But you did. And you started this program everyone thought was crazy, but it wasn't. Anyway, there's this thing called cow cuddling. People come out to the ranch, and they get to...spend time with the cattle. I've been teaching them to lay down and let me 'cuddle' into them." He made air quotes around the word cuddle, and Karla thought he'd done a great job explaining what they did with the cows in the pasture.

Sissy glanced around, a dubious look on her face. "And people pay for this," she said.

"Yeah," he said.

"They pay a lot," Amber said. She turned her phone toward Sissy, where she had the website Karla had built pulled up. Pride flashed through her. That was one good-looking website, if she did say so herself.

"Three hundred dollars?" Sissy abandoned her food then to take the phone from Amber. "A new wellness trend," she read. "Two people. Ninety minutes. Fascinating." She handed the phone back to Amber. "And we want to do this at Last Chance Ranch?"

"Yes," Adele and Cache said at the same time. "It brings in money for the ranch, and people learn about what we do here. We can send them over to volunteer, or to adopt animals, and they get to learn about cattle."

"They brush them down," Cache said. "I teach them a little about the cows. They get to pet them, play with them, and cuddle—if they want." He cut a glance at Karla, and she wondered if she was supposed to say something. They hadn't rehearsed this part. He'd asked her to be there when he talked to Sissy, because he was nervous he might forget something.

But he hadn't.

"And you need money to start? Is that why you need to talk to me?"

"We need an account, yes," Cache said. "We've already got registrations. But we need an account set up for us, and we'll put in a budget, all of that."

Sissy smiled at him kindly and lifted her spoon to her mouth. After swallowing, she said, "You have no idea what 'all of that' means, do you?"

"No clue," he said with a grin.

Karla laughed with the others, putting her hand on Cache's knee. He swung his full attention to her then, and she smiled at him in what she hoped was an encouraging way.

"Come over to my office whenever," Sissy said. "I'll get you what you need, and we'll go over it."

"Great." He beamed at her, collected his folder of

information, and got up. Karla followed suit, her heart lighter than it had been in such a long time.

She cleaned up, glad when Hudson and Ames stayed to help take down the tables and tents. With everything put away and Karla back inside her air-conditioned house, she tipped her head toward heaven and said, "Thank you, Lord."

And for the first time in almost a decade, she actually felt Him smiling down upon her. It was the most wonderful feeling in the world, and Karla wanted to hold onto it forever.

And Cache. She wanted to hold onto him forever too, and the thought actually scared her a little bit.

After all, if she really wanted him in her life, their relationship couldn't stay secret forever. And that meant people would know. They'd ask questions. She'd have to give answers.

"Can I really get married again?" she asked herself. Maybe she was asking God. She wasn't sure, and she didn't know the answer.

Chapter Fifteen

Cache entered the church first on Sunday, his palms hurting from where the rope had slipped during that morning's chores. He was tired of leaving Karla in the truck and hoping she'd follow him inside, found the whole ruse almost unethical.

He knew they weren't hurting anyone, and he wasn't really lying about anything. He spotted Dave sitting alone, which was odd as he'd had Sissy with him for weeks now. Not only that, but Dave seemed relentless in his pursuit to find out what Cache was doing all the time and if he liked Karla or not.

He'd admitted it to Lance, but he'd denied things to Dave over and over. But, in order to keep up the charade of not dating Karla, he walked down the aisle to where Dave sat. "Is there room for me?" he asked, mentally calculating that there was enough space for him *and* Karla.

"Sure." Dave moved down and Cache sat on the end, pressing his hands together to try to get the sting out. Sometimes the rescue dogs on the ranch got spooked, and that was exactly what had happened with Bulldozer today while Cache had him on a lead.

He'd held on a little too long, his skin getting burned until his brain caught up to the situation. Then he'd dropped the rope and managed to stomp on it before Bulldozer got too far away.

The Fourth of July celebration and dog adoption event was in two days, and Cache wanted to give as many dogs as possible a new home, Bulldozer included. So he'd been taking the dogs out in groups to get them away from the compound and comfortable out in the open. They'd been doing really great—until that morning.

"Is there room here?" Karla asked, and Cache glanced up at her.

"Yeah." He got to his feet and stepped out into the aisle so Karla could sit between him and Dave. Dave inched down a little, smiling at Karla and giving Cache a knowing look. Thankfully, he didn't say anything.

Sitting in church with Karla so close and not being able to hold her hand usually tortured Cache. Today, it actually annoyed him. He folded his arms and focused his attention up front, hoping Pastor Williams would have some wise words for him this morning.

He spoke about the unfathomable love of the Lord, and Cache allowed himself to get caught up in the man's deep voice. He relaxed, finally finding his center after a long week of sneaking out late and getting up early to get chores done quicker so he and Karla could have a private hour in the pastures too.

His phone buzzed, breaking his attention, and Cache pulled it out of his shirt pocket to see Dave's name on the screen.

She's crying.

Cache looked over at his friend—and saw that Karla was indeed crying. His first instinct was to put his arm around her and whisper all the same condolences he had a month ago. But he hesitated.

Before he could decide what to do, she got to her feet and said, "Excuse me," as she stepped over him without waiting for him to get up and let her out. He looked back up front as if the pastor would stop his sermon because of Karla's departure, and then looked at Dave.

"Better go after her," Dave said quietly, and Cache didn't think this time. He just went after Karla.

A call flashed on his phone, which he still held in his hand, and he glanced at it. His brother. He looked left and right, the vibrations from the call moving up his forearm as he hurried out of the chapel.

In the lobby, he couldn't see Karla and he swiped on the call at the same time. "Leo," he said in a hushed tone, his legs still taking him quickly toward the exit.

The sunshine outside almost seemed oppressive, and Cache's eyes squinted as a natural response. Dang, Karla could move fast when she wanted to. She'd never run out of church before—well, at least not after that first time. But he'd expected that, and he'd already been on his feet to follow her.

He'd reacted too slowly this time, and he had no idea where she'd gone. Surely not back to the truck, which was parked on black asphalt and would be boiling hot inside. He had the keys. She couldn't just leave.

"Cache?"

He realized he was on the phone with his brother. Blinking, he said, "Yeah, I'm here."

"What do you think?"

"I didn't hear you," he said, still distracted. "Say it again?"

"I said Dad has been seeing someone, and they've gotten serious. He wants you to come out here and meet her."

A sticky feeling coated his throat, and Cache didn't know what to say. He'd lost his mother when he was only a teenager, and his father had never dated. Never tried to find someone else. He'd been a good dad, working hard on the dairy farm and taking care of Cache and Leo. It had been the three of them for so long, Cache wasn't sure there was room for anyone else.

"Yeah," he finally said, moving over to the shade of the tree in front of the church. "When?"

"He's thinking next month. We're always here, but he's not sure what your schedule is like."

Cache rubbed his free hand over his face, not wanting to think about anything today. He didn't want to go back to the ranch and do more chores. Didn't want to worry about the cow cuddling that began that weekend.

That weekend.

Panic gripped his gut, but he kept it from rising through his throat. "That should be fine," he said. "Let me look at my schedule and talk to my boss."

"Sure," Leo said easily. "I think you'll really like Brenda."

"You think so?" Cache asked.

"I do," Leo said. "I've met her several times. She's nice, and she has two grown daughters. She's really good for Dad."

"That's great," Cache said, but he wasn't entirely sure if that was true or not. But Leo and their father had moved to Shiloh Ridge together two years ago while Cache had chosen to come west. He didn't see his father all that often, but they kept in touch with texts and calls.

He was closer to Leo, and he'd always trusted his younger brother. "What about you?" he asked. "Are you seeing anyone?"

Leo burst out laughing, which brought a smile to Cache's face. "I'll take that as a no," he said while his brother continued to chuckle.

"It's a no," Leo said. He didn't ask if Cache was dating anyone, and Cache wasn't surprised. He wasn't exactly known in the family as a ladies man. He asked about the cows instead, and Cache told him about the cow cuddling and how they were starting in six short days.

They talked for several minutes, and when people started exiting the church behind him, Cache said he had to go. He'd lost his private window of opportunity to find Karla, and he glanced around, wondering what to do.

He looked down at his phone and decided to call her, praying she'd pick up. Thankfully, she did, and he asked, "Hey. How are—? Church is over."

"Who called?" she asked.

Cache frowned, his brain moving fast but seemingly so slow at the same time. "My brother."

"I'm coming." She hung up, and Cache had no idea what to expect when he came face-to-face with her again. He turned back toward the church and caught sight of her coming around it from the side. So she'd been able to see him standing there in the shade on his phone.

She didn't look like she'd been crying. Not a single hair sat out of place, and her makeup looked as flawless as ever. She reached for his hand as she said, "They were happy tears, Cache."

"I'm glad." They walked toward his truck, Karla dropping his hand on the second step as if she'd realized she shouldn't be holding his hand in public.

He got behind the wheel and waited for her to get in on her side. She never slid over and rode next to him when they went to church, and Cache sighed. "I'm getting tired of the games," he said.

Karla nodded. "I know."

He waited for her say more, but she didn't. That was it. She knew he didn't like it, but she had no solution. Cache didn't have one either, for that matter. So he drove her back to her cabin and then he disappeared into his, wondering if he'd see her later or not.

THAT EVENING, he left his cabin with plenty of light left in the day. No, he hadn't heard from Karla. No, he wasn't going to her house. He hadn't talked to Scarlett about time off. He was going to water his cows and get them to lie down so he could find some peace.

He stepped through the gate and got to work rinsing out the trough and filling it with clear, crisp, cold water. So cold it hurt his hands when he rinsed them and faced the twelve cows in the pasture.

He'd move six of them to a different field when he and Karla did their cuddling sessions.

With a flash of panic, he wondered if she'd still do them with him. They hadn't exactly had a fight. He wasn't even sure what was broken between them, only that he felt himself moving farther from her now instead of getting closer.

"Hey, Cookie," he said to the cow ambling toward him. She drank, and Cache stepped out of the way as several more joined her. Genuine happiness touched his heart, and a soft smile appeared on his lips.

He loved these cows, as stupid as that might seem. They never tried to hide anything from him, and they relied on him to take care of them. He patted Bluebell on the rump and moved away. "Hurry up, guys. We have training to do."

Peering toward the far end of the pasture, he found the four cows that never really came down while a human was in the field with them. He'd move them tomorrow, back in with the rest of the herd. He had enough cows trained for cuddling sessions, and there was no sense in making a stubborn cow do what it didn't want to do.

He moved over to the right, where he and Karla had been bedding down the cows, and he got six of them into a formation in only ten minutes. They stayed right where he put them, and Cache beamed down at them.

Closing his eyes, he imagined twelve people in this field with him. He'd give them a ten-minute orientation outside the fence before they even came in. Then they'd stay by the trough while he talked to them about the cows and showed them how he got them to lay down. Then they'd get to cuddle with the bovines, and at the end, they'd have a chance to pet them, brush them, and ask questions.

Please let it work out, he prayed. With all that extra money every month, he could be out of debt and ready to face a brighter future in no time at all.

"A future with Karla?" he murmured, reaching for his phone. She might want things between them to fade away or never make it out of the shadows. But that was not what Cache wanted, and he kept praying as her line rang. And rang. And rang.

Chapter Sixteen

Karla stepped out of the shower when the water started running colder. She'd been so cold all day, and she couldn't figure out why.

Fine, she'd only caught the chill after church, after she'd felt the spirit of God so close to her it had brought tears to her eyes. The sense of forgiveness flowing through her as Pastor Williams had spoken about the Lord's love for her had been utterly overwhelming.

His love goes beyond anything you might have done, the pastor had said. *He is always there, waiting to welcome you back. His plea to "Come, follow me," never expires. It is not conditional. He does not call only the righteous to his side, but all of us.*

Karla heard her phone ringing in the kitchen, but she ignored it. She wanted to write down the pastor's words before they left her head. An impossibility, as they'd been circling in her brain for hours now.

Still, she took the time to scrawl them into a notebook she kept beside her bed, reading over them and touching the words *all of us* as fresh tears burned her eyes.

Blinking them back, she stood to get dressed at the same time someone knocked on her back door.

Banging would've been a better way to describe it. She jumped, her adrenaline sending her pulse into a frenzy.

And when Cache called, "Karla, it's me," she ran on her tiptoes to the door and closed it, as if he'd come inside without her permission. With her phone in the kitchen and a towel as her only clothing, she couldn't communicate with him right now.

So she flung the towel off and dressed as quickly as she could. It still took a few minutes, and by the time she snagged her phone from the kitchen and hurried to the back door, she could only hope he hadn't left in a rage.

Cache wasn't really the ragey type, and she wasn't all that surprised to see him sitting on her back steps, muttering to himself.

"Hey, sorry," she said.

He sprang to his feet and turned toward her, a perfect storm of emotions on that handsome face.

"I was in the shower when you called." She lifted her phone. "And, uh, you knocked while I was still...I wasn't dressed." She reached up and touched the towel turban still on her head, as if he needed evidence that she had indeed been in the shower.

He glanced left and right. "I hope you're not mad I came in the daylight."

"Come in," she said, backing out of the doorway.

He did, and Karla sure liked the presence of him in her cabin, and in her life. "I didn't get over to the pasture yet."

"I did," he said. "I got all the cows down and I called to see if you wanted to come and cuddle with me." He touched her hand, and she turned into him. "We're okay, right?" he asked, drawing her into his arms.

"Yeah," she said, everything in her life suddenly more than okay. "I'm sorry about...everything." She tipped her head back and looked up at him. "I know you don't want us to be a secret anymore, but I kinda like having a secret sweetheart."

He grinned down at her, and that hungry look in his eye said he liked it on some level too. He bent down and kissed her, but this wasn't one of his rougher, passionate kisses. It definitely held a level of love and adoration she'd never felt before, because he moved slowly, as if he wanted to savor each moment.

She felt drunk on his touch, and when he finally pulled away, Karla kept her eyes closed as her awareness spun.

"I like our privacy too," he said. "But people are asking about us, and I don't get why I can't just tell them."

"Who's asking?" she asked. No one had said anything to her, but she spent most of her time alone, in her cabin, working. Or in a large groups as she fed the workers on the ranch.

"Dave," Cache said. "He knows, though I've denied it. And Lance."

Of course. The men he spent a lot of time with. His friends. Of course they knew. Cache's whole routine had changed since they'd started seeing one another.

He ran his lips across her jaw, sending a shiver through her whole system. "I don't want to deny it anymore," he said. "I really like you, Karla."

She held onto those powerful shoulders for dear life, because she really liked him too. "I'm almost there," she said. "I swear."

"So a little longer." The man could work magic with that mouth, and Karla sighed as she nodded.

"A little longer."

A COUPLE OF DAYS LATER, she worked all morning in the kitchen to put out lunch for the ranch. Forever Friends would be feeding everyone that night as part of the tri-sponsored holiday event, but their traditional Fourth of July ranch luncheon was still happening.

Adele manned the grill each year, but Karla had taken over all of the condiments for the burgers, as well as a variety of salads to go with them. The dessert bar was a potluck, and when she finally stepped out her front door with two big silver bowls of salad—on potato and one macaroni—she found the tents and tables already set up.

She was running late, because she'd been texting Cache's brother Leo about his upcoming birthday.

Just two weeks away, Karla wanted to do something special for him. For her, that meant food, brownies, cakes, balloons. Maybe she'd fill his whole house with balloons while he fed and watered dogs, shoed horses, and then cuddled with cows.

The very thought brought a smile to her lips. Leo had been very helpful, and she had a good idea of how to surprise Cache on his birthday.

Six desserts sat on one of the serving tables, and she hurried to put her heavy salad bowls down next to them. She'd made a green salad too, as well as one with cherry gelatin.

"Smells good," she said to Adele, who stood at the smoky grill. She smiled at Karla and flipped another couple of burgers.

Karla returned with the rest of her salads, as well as serving tongs, forks, and spoons. Several people milled about, but the party didn't start until Adele called everyone over.

"I think we know the drill. You load up on what you want over there, and tell me what protein you want. I have some burgers at medium, and some at medium-well. Some with cheese and some without."

Karla's mouth watered at the scent of hot dogs—there was nothing better than a good hot dog in her opinion—and she stepped next to Amber as Adele finished her speech.

The two women exchanged a glance and a smile as Scarlett said a few words about how grateful she was to have everyone there. "Our first lunch was so much smaller than this." She sniffled, and leaned into Hudson with a brilliant smile. "We really are so glad to have you all here with us every year. You are our family."

Cache appeared at her side, and Karla only half-twisted toward him. He slipped his hand into her and leaned in to kiss her, and it felt like every eye within a hundred miles zeroed in on them.

She pulled in a breath, her gaze immediately flying to Scarlett, who had stopped talking. She was staring at Karla and Cache, her eyes a little wider than they'd been a moment ago.

"Carson's going to say a prayer, and then we'll eat," Hudson said, seemingly nonplussed about Cache's public display of affection.

He inched away from her as if he'd realized what he'd just done. Karla still couldn't believe it. They'd just talked about their secret relationship a couple of days ago. Had he completely lost his mind?

She didn't hear a word of the prayer, and her insides

quivered as if they'd been set in gelatin and then been shaken up.

"Amen," everyone chorused when the prayer ended, but Karla remained mute. She looked at Cache, and he wore guilt all over his face before stepping away.

"Are you dating Cache?" Amber asked, and Karla wanted to crawl in a hole and cover herself with dirt. Before she could even answer, Scarlett appeared in front of her.

"You and Cache?"

Karla could only shake her head, but she didn't even know what that meant. No, she wasn't dating Cache? She sure did kiss the man a lot, and think about him constantly, and cook for him more than was healthy if they weren't dating.

"She doesn't want to talk about it," Adele said, a greasy spatula in her hand. Karla met her eyes, gratitude streaming through her. "So, Karla, here's a question you might have an easier time answering. Hamburger or hot dog?"

"Hot dog," she managed to say, ducking her head so her long hair fell between her and the rest of the women. She took her dog and moved over to the table to get the salads and desserts she wanted.

When she turned and faced the tables, Cache had an empty spot next to him. She swallowed, suddenly so nervous. She had to sit by him. She couldn't snub him that way. Didn't even want to.

Before she could take a single step, Scarlett sat beside him, with Hudson across from her. Relief spread through Karla, and she went over to the table and sat beside Hudson, a quick smile in Cache's direction.

He barely looked at her, and Scarlett said, "We'll need all hands on-deck to move the animals down to the church this afternoon."

Karla didn't know who she was talking to, but several of the cowboys said they'd be around to help. Karla dug into the macaroni salad, hoping she could quell the jittery feeling in her stomach with carbs.

The mood surrounding her felt so foreign, though she normally loved the Fourth of July picnic at the ranch. In fact, it had been the highlight of her year last time. But she felt like she existed on the other side of a clear barrier. Inside a balloon, where the laughter couldn't reach her ears.

People could see her, sure. She could hear them. But she couldn't get herself to participate, and her smile felt fake all the way back in her mouth.

But she kept it on her face, got up when everyone seemed finished, and started cleaning up. If she kept busy and around people, she wouldn't have to face Cache.

At least that was what she told herself.

Chapter Seventeen

Cache loitered as long as he dared, but Karla didn't glance in his direction once. He supposed he had hidden in the shadows along the side of the house. For one, it was too hot to stand out in the sun. And two, he wanted to gauge how upset Karla was.

By the looks of it, she was pretty upset. Cache was too, for that matter. He should be able to step next to her and press his lips to her temple. He hadn't done anything scandalous, but he'd seen the way the women on the ranch had descended on Karla.

And he knew she hated that.

His phone buzzed, and he turned away from her curvy form as she took another few plates up the steps and into her house. He had a ton of work to do at the Canine Club to get the dogs ready for transport down to the church and the adoption event in just a few hours.

Sure enough, Hudson had texted to find out where he was and to let him know they were all waiting for him at the Club. Cache put his head down and wished he could turn off his thoughts, but they kept streaming through his mind like water out of a broken faucet.

They needed carriers, and the list of dogs Cache had put together, and a dozen other things. He put in the code to the door and stepped through it. The octagonal buildings spread out before him, the first one only a few paces inside the gate.

He entered it and found Hudson and a few other volunteers standing there. "Hey, everyone," he said. "Sorry I'm a little behind you all." He stepped into the tiny office just inside the front door where he managed the care and feeding of the canines. "I have our adoption list right here."

He glanced at the five or six people looking at him. "We're going to need more people. I know Adele has a list like this in Feline Frenzy too."

"We'll get started," Hudson said. "Forever Friends has people down at the church ready to take over the dogs for us as soon as we get them down there."

"All right," Cache said with a big sigh. "Hudson, I'm going to give you building five." He tugged a sheet free with the six dogs from building five that would be going down to the adopt-a-pet events tonight.

Hudson took the paper with a quick smile, and Cache continued handing out the assignments until he was left with three buildings for himself. He worked, luring the dogs into the kennels and heaving as many as would fit into the back of his truck.

He drove down to the church and unloaded the canines into the large area the Forever Friends volunteers had set up for the dogs.

Four trips later, his back hurt and he'd been sweating for an hour. But all the dogs were in the pen, and the Forever Friends volunteers stood waiting for the details on the animals he'd brought down.

"I think we're just waiting for Adele," he said, glancing around for her. She pulled up as if Cache saying her name had summoned her. She unloaded the last three cats from the back of her car and came toward him.

She looked just as hot as he felt, and he smiled at her. He handed over a thick folder with the one-sheet information on all fifty dogs they'd brought down today. Adele had brought down forty cats, and she gave a longer speech than he did.

Dave came over and took a couple of the more excitable dogs from Hudson, saying, "Let's go, guys," he said to the pups. Cache wished he could take the dogs and leave the crowd, but Dave looked like he needed the break too.

So he answered any questions about the dogs the volunteers had, and he noticed Lance standing a little too close to Amber as she manned the main adoption table. Her being there made sense. Forever Friends actually paid her salary. She was only stationed at Last Chance Ranch, and like Sissy, Amber lived down in Pasadena somewhere. And Lance was totally making a move on the volunteer coordinator for all the animal adoptions on the rescue ranch.

Cache finished with the dog adoptions and turned, wondering if he could escape back up to the ranch and the sanctuary of his cabin. Karla wouldn't be there; she'd committed to helping serve the dinner provided by the church that night.

Food started showing up, and he caught sight of her blonde hair as she helped organize people and plates. The pastor started the event about ten minutes later, and once again Cache found himself loitering on the outskirts of Karla's attention.

She did glance around a couple of times, but she never saw him standing over by the big tree where she'd gone a few times after church. Quite a few people had come to the event, and the atmosphere was fun, and shiny, and lively.

In any other situation, Cache would've been one of the first through the line. He'd have shaken hands with the pastor and grinned at the kids as they ran around. He'd be eyeing a dog to take home later and hoping he'd get to kiss Karla while the red, white, and blue fireworks popped overhead.

She finally went through the line and settled at a table with several other people from the ranch. He might as well face her in a crowd. Get their first interaction since his flub that day out of the way.

He put food on his plate without really seeing it and shook hands with the pastor without focus. He sat at the table across from Karla, and their eyes met.

He wanted to blurt out how sorry he was. That he honestly hadn't thought before stepping up to her and doing what he'd done dozens times before. Dave sat heavily in the seat next to Cache before he could say anything. He had a gray bulldog with him, and he asked, "I'm not interrupting, am I?"

"Nope," Karla said, her tone filled with ice. Cache wanted to take his plate and leave, but he didn't need to cause a bigger scene than he already had.

He glanced at Dave, but Cache focused on his food like he hadn't eaten in days.

"I'm sorry," Dave said, getting up. "I have to go."

"Go?" Cache said after him, because if he left, Cache would be left alone with Karla. But Dave walked away, the bulldog obediently at his side.

"He and Sissy aren't getting along," Karla said as if Cache cared.

He looked at her. "I know how that feels."

"She went to San Diego to visit her family, and he didn't want to go with her."

Cache tilted his head and looked at Karla, trying to figure her out. "You would be so upset if someone was talking about you like this," he said. "Why are you doing it?"

Anger flashed in her eyes, but she didn't try to defend herself. She pushed a few mayo-slathered pieces of potato around on her plate.

"I'm sorry," Cache said. "I really am. I didn't think."

"That much was obvious."

Cache didn't know what to say. She'd said she was getting closer to being able to admit they were together, but Cache felt like they'd taken ten giant steps backward.

"I saw Scarlett and Amber talking to you. I'm sorry," he said again.

"Adele saved me," Karla said, tucking her hair and finally spearing one chunk of potato and putting it in her mouth.

Cache didn't like that she needed to be saved from talking about their relationship. In fact, it sent a popping wave of fury through him. "You know what? I'm going to go too."

"Cache," she said. "Don't go."

He paused, thinking he must like getting tortured. Because he stayed. He didn't look away from Karla as she glanced around to see if anyone was watching them. Another couple from their church congregation sat down at the end of the table, but most people had finished eating and had laid out blankets in front of a blow-up screen where a children's movie was playing.

Karla finally looked at him, apparently satisfied that no

one was watching them. "I know you're not happy with me."

"No," he said. "I'm not." He sighed, some of his frustration leaking out with the words. "Look, Karla, why don't I just make this easy for you? It's okay. You don't want to be with me. It's fine." He started to stand, but Karla put her hands on his.

"I don't want to break up," she said. "Stay." She held up her hand and waited as she stood. Cache liked the bright glint in her eye, and he stayed.

She hurried around the table and stepped right into Cache's arms. "I want to claim you publicly." She tipped up onto her toes and kissed him, right there in front of everyone. Everyone looking, at least, but Cache wasn't sure who that was.

Because he was busy kissing Karla, his not-so-secret girlfriend.

She pulled away with a giggle and placed both her hands on the sides of his face. "I'm really sorry, Cache," she said. "But I think you're right. I don't see why we can't be together."

"Finally," Cache said, wondering what had made her change her mind. He kissed her again, pulling away quickly. "I brought a blanket. Want to watch the fireworks with me?"

"I thought you'd never ask." She beamed up at him, and Cache chuckled.

He laced his fingers through hers and strolled toward his truck. "What changed your mind?"

"Watching you lurk over by the tree," she said. "I hated that you weren't beside me, and I realized that there's where I wanted you."

Cache opened the passenger door and pulled a blanket off the seat. He and Karla went over to the grassy area where a lot of people had settled. A fair few people were milling around the animals and Amber looked a little frazzled as she tried to work with three people at once.

For a moment, he thought Karla would go help her, but she didn't. They set up on a spare patch of grass, and Cache enjoyed the feel of her in his arms as they settled down.

"Ladies and gentlemen," a woman wearing a bright blue Forever Friends vest said into a microphone. "We've just adopted out our last cat!"

A cheer when up, and Cache joined them, hoping that the last of the secrets between him and Karla had finally come out.

Chapter Eighteen

"Yes," Karla said into the phone, glancing at the clock. She was supposed to be in the cow cuddling pasture in two minutes and she still didn't have her shoes on. "Leo, I have to go."

"Just make sure you don't make carrot cake," Cache's brother said. "He hates that stuff. And remember, he acts like he doesn't like surprises, but he does."

"Got it," Karla said. She'd arranged for Leo to call this morning, but he'd had an emergency on his ranch in Shiloh Ridge, and he'd called late. Really late. And Karla hadn't realized what time it was.

She shoved her foot into a shoe as Leo continued to say all the things Cache liked. Karla knew most of them, as she'd been getting to know Cache over the past several weeks. She burst from her cabin and dashed down her steps while Leo was still talking.

At the corner of the road, she said, "Leo, I'll call you back," shoved her phone in her pocket, and hurried toward the entrance gate, where Cache stood with six people.

Three couples.

Their first cow cuddlers.

"Ah, here she is," he said as she approached. He wore worry in his eyes, and she wished she could mentally communicate with him that everything would be fine. They'd decided to cap the sessions at ten people, and two more couples arrived within seconds of one another.

Cache had a whole program outlined before people even went into the pasture, and he launched into it after introducing himself and Karla to the group. She was supposed to answer any questions she could, help get the cows down and in position, and then say good-bye to everyone.

She glanced into the pasture as Cache went over proper etiquette with a bovine, including where not to stand, where not to touch, and to please be aware of surroundings at all times.

"These are wild animals," he said. "I mean, they're domesticated cows. But they're wild animals."

Karla couldn't help smiling at him and his definition of wild animals. "I'm going to go in first," she said. "You can follow me. We ask that you don't move past the trough until we have the cows settled down and ready to cuddle."

Not that the cows in the pasture were rioting or

anything, but Karla still approached the gate first, as if she might encounter rabid lions on the other side.

She moved past the trough and waited for Cache to secure the gate behind him. "If you ever feel uncomfortable," he said. "Come back to the trough. The cows don't come on this side of it."

"Ever?" one of the men asked. He looked like he'd been dragged there by the woman on his arm.

"Ever," Cache said. "They really are trained well, but you're new, and our first session, so anything could happen."

Karla gave him a look, one that said, *Don't say stuff like that*, with her eyes while she kept a smile cemented in place.

Cookie, ever the inquisitive cow, came closer, and Karla turned to her as Cache started detailing what Karla was going to do. Her pulse raced through her body, making her skin and fingertips tingle.

"Come on," she whispered to herself. "Please let this work." She approached Cookie, who usually came the closest first. Their cuddling circle was obvious in the way the grass had been pressed down, and Karla said, "Down," to Cookie, making the hand motion Cache had decided on.

Cookie looked at her for an extra second and then down she went. The excitement from the group behind her was exhilarating, and she called, "Bluebell, Morning Glory, come on."

Cache joined her, rustling up the cattle they needed for this cow cuddling session. They did get six cows situated in a circle, and then Cache brought out each couple one by one and taught them how to cuddle with the cows.

Karla marveled through the whole thing. She hadn't really doubted that it would work, but she had been nervous. But all six cows just laid there, looking bored, while the couples laughed, talked, took selfies, and generally enjoyed themselves. She and Cache fed the cattle small bites of carrots and apples to get them to stay, answered questions, and exchanged a dozen glances.

In short, it was the best morning she'd experienced in a long, long time. Not only that, she had a secret birthday party for Cache on the horizon, and she'd claimed him in front of everyone at the Fourth of July event.

Since then, no one had come to talk to her about her relationship with the bright-eyed, witty cowboy. She wasn't sure why she'd thought they would, or why she'd been so afraid to take their relationship out of the shadows.

She'd imagined all kinds of crazy things in her head, from having to defend her reasons for not wanting to date him then to why he was perfect for her. But Scarlett hadn't asked again, not even over text.

Amber seemed busy with her new boyfriend too, and Adele had plenty to deal with in her high-risk pregnancy. Sissy had returned to the ranch on the night of the Fourth of July, and the next morning, she'd been wearing a diamond ring around. Karla had heard at least ten rumors about Dave and Sissy by lunchtime, and that was why she'd been worried about making her relationship with Cache public.

After all, she had plenty to keep hidden in her past. And her present. She did not need everyone and their dog —literally—talking about her.

Not only that, but Dave and Sissy were going to be married in only five weeks. Well, less than that now. Karla couldn't even imagine such a thing, and her thoughts rotated to her sister and how much planning she'd already done for her big day that was still months away.

Everything muddied in her mind, and she pushed out all of the confusing, rotating thoughts and focused on the cute couples at their very first cow cuddling session. Cache finished up with petting and brushing, and the session ended.

When the last visitor had stepped through the gate and walked back to their car, Cache turned toward her, a look of pure joy and wonder on his face.

"I can't believe it," he said. He grabbed his hat and tossed it up into the air with a whoop, grabbing onto her and spinning her around as he laughed. "That was *great*. Right?"

"Amazing," she said, the high of the last hour and a half still buzzing through her body. "Sissy said we just need to go over to her office, and she'll figure out how to get us paid too."

Cache grinned, his happiness so infectious when he wore it out in the open for everyone to see.

"Thank you, Karla," he said, sobering.

"I didn't do anything, cowboy," she said. "You're the one who made this program a success."

He walked over and picked up his hat. "I can't wait to do it again."

Secretly, Karla couldn't either.

JULY PASSED in a blur of record-breaking heat and cuddling sessions and cooking. If she wasn't making lunch for the ranch, then she did for Cache. No one—not a single person—had said anything to her about dating him, and she wondered if some internal memo had gone around and she didn't know about it.

Probably not. Probably just the excitement of Dave and Sissy's wedding, which was only eight days away now.

Karla had been asked to make the cake, and she'd been going over designs with Sissy for a few days now. It was too hot to feed everyone on the ranch, and Scarlett had started buying pizza once a week for everyone as the ranch prepared for its fourth wedding.

Karla couldn't help wondering if she and Cache would make number five.

She'd made dozens of cakes in the past, and a couple of

weeks after the wedding, she'd be making one for Cache's birthday. Which reminded her....

She picked up her phone despite the flour on her fingers. *Can I use the barn for Cache's birthday?* she typed out in a text to Scarlett.

Sure, Scarlett answered. *But I want a lunch date where you tell me everything that's happened between the two of you as payment.*

Karla thought that was a pretty steep price, and she hesitated to agree. In the end, she did, along with, *It's a surprise. We need a way to let everyone know about it except for him.*

I'll come to lunch with some ideas tomorrow, Scarlett messaged back, and there was no getting around the meal then.

She felt jittery and sick the next morning—about how she'd felt before going to church with Cache for the first time months ago. She set the rolls on the table at the same time Scarlett knocked and then entered—and she wasn't alone.

Adele was with her, as was Sissy herself.

Karla felt absolutely ambushed, especially when she hadn't even said hello yet when another knock sounded. Sissy opened the door and Amber walked in with Jeri and the baby. Brayden stole the spotlight for a few minutes, which was just fine with Karla, who had no idea what to say to her friends.

And she didn't have enough food. She busied herself

pulling another container of turkey chili out of the freezer and sticking it in the microwave. Adele migrated closer to her, and Karla had always liked her next-door neighbor.

"Feeling okay?" she asked.

"Not really," Karla said, glancing at her out of the corner of her eye. "I'm not good with groups."

Laughter rang out behind her, and she turned to face the rest of her house. She had to do this. She couldn't hide from everything anymore, and she couldn't take back the evidence of her relationship with Cache.

"Still planning a trip to help your sister out?" Scarlett asked. "Remind me of those dates again."

"August twenty-fifth through the thirty-first," she said. "Right after Cache's birthday."

"Right." Scarlett swiped on her phone and tapped in the info. "Got it in my calendar now."

"How's the cow cuddling going?" Amber asked, her waves and waves of hair falling over her shoulders in perfect curls. It almost seemed like everyone had agreed on topics before they'd shown up.

Adele with how she was feeling. Scarlett about a trip that had been on the calendar for a couple of months now. And now Amber with the cow cuddling.

The microwave beeped and she pulled out the chili to stir it. "Great," she said. The chili was still frozen and she practically shoved it back into the microwave.

She slammed it closed at the same time her back door

crashed open. "You've been talking to my brother behind my back?"

Cache stood there, and it was clear he'd lost his mind again. Did he not see all the women in her cabin?

He glanced around, seeming to suddenly come to his senses. He said, "I can't believe you," and turned and stormed out as quickly as he'd come in.

Karla stood there, the spoon she'd just used to stir the turkey chili still clutched in her hand.

"You better go after him," Adele said, taking the spoon.

"Now," Scarlett said as the roar of a truck engine filled the air.

Chapter Nineteen

Cache could barely see he was so angry. His tires spit gravel behind him as he pulled away from Karla's cabin. The sight of her in there, laughing with all of those women...it burned. Burned right through him, leaving nothing but smoke and ashes in its wake.

Laughing with them.

"Probably laughing at you," he muttered, slowing to take the corner so he didn't roll his truck. In his back pocket, his phone buzzed. He ignored it. He didn't want to talk to Karla right now, and the likely other person who'd be calling if not for her was Leo.

Leo.

He could not believe she'd been talking to him behind Cache's back. In secret.

But Karla did almost everything in secret—he knew

that. He wasn't sure why he'd expected her to act differently with him.

At his cabin, he left the truck idling and ran inside to pack a bag. He didn't need much. A couple changes of clothes. A few toiletries. His chargers and his laptop. Wallet. Driver's license. Money.

He opened the cupboard above the microwave and pulled down a jar. He'd been cashing all of his cow cuddling checks and keeping the money there. The Lord had blessed him so much this summer, and as Cache stared at the bills, a measure of desperation pulled through him.

Why? ran through his mind, and he hated that question. He'd asked it when so many women had chosen Leo over him. When his mother had died. When they'd lost the dairy farm. When Karla wanted to keep everything about their relationship a secret.

He grabbed a handful of bills and folded them into his pocket. Another handful went in his wallet. He turned to leave, hoping he'd been fast enough to get away from the ranch without having to face Karla directly.

A knock sounded on the door before he could put the jar with the remaining money back. He hurried to do so and strode toward the more urgent sound as it happened again. He knew who would be there, and he didn't want to talk.

Had had enough talking.

Enough lies.

Enough secrets.

He grabbed his suitcase and opened the door. Karla stood there, wringing her hands. She took him in from the top of his cowboy hat to the suitcase in his hands. "You're leaving?"

"They need my help in Shiloh Ridge," he said, brushing past her and heading for the idling truck. She'd parked behind him, though, and unless he wanted to bash in her car, he wasn't leaving until she did.

He automatically started calculating how sharp his truck could turn and how well it would handle on the baked earth that sometimes had green grass between his place and Lance's. But with it being August now, everything was dry and hard, and Cache suspected he could get out of the driveway by going off-road for a moment.

And he would. He'd do whatever it took to get away from this pain. This betrayal.

"I called Leo to plan a surprise birthday party," Karla called after him as he swung his suitcase into the back of his truck. He hadn't lied. Leo had called to tell him about an emergency on the ranch. He'd even asked Cache's opinion, and that hadn't happened very often in their lives.

"I don't like surprises," he said over his shoulder. He turned back to face her, deciding he had to say what was on his mind. He should get to, even if it upset her. Even if it drove them apart. She'd done what she wanted throughout the relationship, and while her beauty made him ache, he deserved to have an active role in their relationship too.

But there wasn't going to be a relationship for much longer.

"Karla, I said this at the Fourth, and I'm going to say it again. It's okay if we can't be together. I'm fine. You're fine. And it's obviously not working."

"I'm not fine," she said.

"Well, I'm real sorry about that." He rounded the front of the truck, pausing next to the rear-view mirror and looking at her across the hood. "But I'm done. I don't like the secrets, the surprises, the cabin full of giggling women. You keep too many secrets for me."

He moved to open the door, surprised when she opened the passenger side as if she'd get into the truck with him. She didn't, but she kept one hand on the door while she leaned into the cab. "I told you everything."

"You didn't tell me you'd snuck my phone to get my brother's number." He didn't care what they were talking about. He should've known she was conversing with his brother.

"Ask Leo. He'll tell you I was just asking about you, about what you'd like for your birthday." She sounded furious and frustrated, but Cache just wanted to tell her to join the club.

"Karla, those are things you should've known already about me." He looked at her. Didn't she understand? "I've had enough secrets. Your past, then us, then all the texts and phone calls. I don't think you even realize how much you've been talking to him behind my back."

He couldn't help the insecurities and jealousy that washed over him. They pounded against him like relentless ocean waves, and he started the truck. He had to leave. Now.

"I've had enough. Who knows what you'll keep secret next?"

"Nothing," she said, her chin quivering.

"Oh, just the birthday party," he said. "And then it'll be something else. And then some*one* else."

He shouldn't have said it. He knew the moment he did it had been a mistake. But he couldn't take it back, and so much pain radiated through him that he couldn't apologize for it.

"I have to go," he said. "My flight leaves soon."

"Cache, don't go," she said. "I love you."

The words gave him a moment's pause, and then he shoved them away. "Well, I don't love you. It's over, Karla."

He put the truck in drive, and she fell back, her face pale and broken. As Cache maneuvered onto the dry lawn and down Lance's driveway, he knew he *had* just lied.

Because he didn't have a flight to catch yet—and he *was* in love with Karla Jenkins.

"I'll be back for the wedding," he said to Dave an hour later. The Long Beach Airport was light and airy, and he liked the coziness of the terminal. It smelled like cinnamon and sugar, and he'd eaten a cinnamon roll as soon as he'd secured a ticket to Denver.

"It's next week," Dave said.

"I know when it is." The forthcoming nuptials were all Dave could talk about, and Cache had agreed that their band would play for the reception—minus Dave. They were doing slower ballads, all instrumental, as their lead singer would be the one tying the knot.

"What's really going on?" Dave asked.

"My brother needs help for a couple of days." And he'd been planning to go meet his dad's girlfriend this fall anyway. Sure, it was a little sooner than he'd planned, but did that really matter? Did he have to explain everything he did?

Probably, when his absence at Last Chance Ranch affected others. "Look, I just need help covering my chores for a few days," he said. "I'll ask Carson to take over in the Canine Club, but can you make sure the cows are watered every day? It doesn't even have to be in the morning. I'll talk to Gina or Hudson about the horses."

"Why can't Karla water the cows?" Dave asked. "Isn't she out there with you anyway? And what about cow cuddling?"

Cache sighed, feeling like someone had put the world on his shoulders and was now pressing down. "I'll ask

Karla about the cows," he said, just to prove that he was still talking to her. "Can you do the stuff in Horse Heaven?"

"Yeah," Dave said. "But Cache, if something—"

"Dave, I don't want to talk about anything else. I have to go." He hung up without waiting for his friend to agree and gripped the phone like he could strangle it somehow. Make it stop bothering him with buzzes and bleeps.

He texted Scarlett and said he had a family emergency. That was barely bordering on true, but he felt frantic inside over Karla and Leo's messages and phone calls, so he thought he could get away with the classification.

His flight finally boarded, and he waited until the plane started moving before he sent a quick message to Karla. *Please water the cows while I'm gone. I'll be back Sunday. Cancel the classes between now and then if you want to.*

That gave him four days in Shiloh Ridge, and he had no idea if that would be long enough to figure out how to live and work at Last Chance Ranch when he couldn't have Karla.

He turned his phone to airplane mode and leaned his head back, the pressure still heavy against his shoulders at the thought of seeing Karla and not being able to kiss her.

HE SPOTTED his father through the crowds, because the man was so tall and wore a huge, white cowboy hat. Nerves danced through him, as he hadn't seen Leo or his dad in about a year, and the thought of having to meet someone who could potentially become his step-mother had kept him awake on the plane when all he'd wanted to do was sleep.

"Dad," he said, hurrying the last few steps to him. They embraced, and Cache felt all his troubles disappear. His dad had been everything to him for such a long time.

"Cache." His dad held him tight and clapped him on the back a few times. "The flight was okay?"

"Great," Cache said, readjusting his backpack after he stepped back. Leo hadn't come, and Cache was half-happy and half-upset that his brother had respected his wishes.

"This is Brenda Merchant," his dad said, stepping to the side of a brunette that barely went to his dad's chest. She wore a brilliant smile, and his father tucked her against his side as if he'd done so many times in the past.

She had a good spirit about her, and all of Cache's nerves settled. "Brenda," he said. "It's so nice to meet you." He accepted her hug, taking an extra moment to see how he felt.

And it sure did feel good to have the embrace of a mother once more. He hadn't realized how much he craved such a thing until that moment, and he held her a little tighter for a little longer.

Feeling a touch awkward, he finally stepped back. "Is this the car?"

"Yep," his dad said, still watching him. "Is that all you've got?"

"Yep," Cache said, lifting his single suitcase into the trunk. "Let's go." He didn't really want to see Leo yet, but he would like to see all the cows they'd brought to the ranch here.

Shiloh Ridge sat in Three Rivers, Texas, a growing town surrounded by ranches and farms, and that was about an hour from the airport in Amarillo. They filled the time with easy conversation, and Cache could see why his dad liked Brenda so much. Leo too.

She was soft and kind. She laughed easily. She told great stories about her daughters and her life in Shiloh Ridge and the neighboring town of Three Rivers.

Cache wasn't sure what that meant, but by the time his dad navigated them through the quaint little town and up into the foothills again, darkness was starting to gather. Brenda tried pointing out all the shops as she told little snippets of Christmas traditions in the town, but Cache couldn't really see them.

Cache had never been so exhausted, but he said he didn't mind when his dad asked if they could drop Brenda off at her place in town first. Once she'd vacated the front seat, Cache took it, and he said, "I think I'll head straight to bed when we get to the ranch, if that's okay."

"Should be fine," his dad said. "Long day for you."

"Yeah." Cache had never liked traveling all that much, and he sure hoped he could find a way to turn off his thoughts long enough to get some rest.

"So we'll talk about Karla in the morning," his dad said, causing Cache to twist toward him.

"I don't think so, Dad."

"Hmm," his dad said, and that meant, yes, they'd be talking about Karla in the morning.

Chapter Twenty

Karla couldn't believe Cache had left Last Chance Ranch. But she'd seen him make a U-turn over the grass. Rumble on down the road. Drive right past the robot mailbox and disappear from sight.

She couldn't go back to her cabin and face everyone. Not with tears streaming down her face and the worst words in the world refusing to leave her mind.

Well, I don't love you.

She'd never had to doubt how Cache felt about her. He said things in words, while she was the one who showed him how she felt by cooking, baking, watering the cows, and spending time with him.

Couldn't he see that her texts and calls to Leo weren't bad? Yes, she'd taken his phone one day a while ago while he was in the bathroom. She'd put his brother's number in her phone so she could get the inside scoop on Cache.

Those are things you should've known already about me.

Maybe he was right.

"Of course he was right," Karla murmured to herself. She left her car in Cache's driveway and wandered down the road to the pasture where she'd found so much relief this summer. Not physical relief from the sun. Not the spiritual and emotional relief she'd found at church. But the mental relief she needed from worrying about her past, what people thought of her, what they might be saying about her.

She rinsed out the trough though it looked like it had already been done for the day. Then she filled it with fresh, crisp water and turned toward the cows.

Bluebell had wandered closer to her today, and Karla gave the cow a shaky smile. "Down, girl," she said, and she barely gave Bluebell time to get situated before she curled into her side.

Karla cried then, behind the wall of cow flesh separating her from the rest of the ranch. Bluebell didn't flinch, and she didn't try to tell her everything would be okay. Strangely, Karla was able to feel that way on her own, and she looked up in the sky to see if heaven had opened.

It hadn't, of course, but she still felt calmer than she had in a long, long time. She had a foundation from which she could work, and she hadn't had something that strong since coming to California.

She pulled out her phone and called Wendy, hoping her sister would be able to talk for a few minutes.

"Can I call you back in ten minutes?" Wendy answered, and Karla said, "Sure," and hung up. Wendy worked in retail management, and with it being August now, the back-to-school shopping would be in full swing.

"What should I do, Bluebell?" she asked the cow. "Cache can be so stubborn sometimes." So she'd kept some secrets. It wasn't like he didn't have any. Everyone had secrets. And she'd only talked to Leo to plan a surprise. Why was this such a big deal to him?

As if someone had cracked open her skull and poured knowledge into her brain, she realized what she'd done.

She'd been sneaking around behind his back—at least in his eyes. And with the worst person possible. His brother.

He'd told her about the girl he'd had a crush on earlier in his life, and how she'd chosen Leo over him.

"So maybe he's sensitive about that."

But he'd also told her he trusted her. That he didn't believe she'd cheat on him—and she hadn't. Didn't. Wouldn't.

"But how can I make him understand that?" Even as she asked the cow the question, she knew the answer. She couldn't *make* anyone understand anything. Wars were fought trying to do that, and political careers made and broken.

So she wouldn't be able to get a cowboy to believe

anything. Yes, Cache was generally easy-going, but Karla had learned over the months that his joviality was what he allowed others to see.

He was like an iceberg, with only the best part of him showing above the surface of the water. But underneath, he was craggly, and deep, and complex—and Karla had spoken true. She loved him. Every part of that buried iceberg and all of his complications.

"I need to get him back," she said, her mind already whirring. "How long do you think he'll stay away from the ranch?"

Of course, Bluebell didn't know, and a series of texts came through her phone. Scarlett, wondering where she was and if she was coming back. Wendy, saying she'd need a few more minutes until she could call.

You should see what I just broke up, she said, causing a smile to cross Karla's face. Gratitude also moved through her that she didn't have to clean up dressing rooms, deal with frazzled moms trying to get the best deal, or report thieves to mall security.

"Thank you," she whispered to the sky, hoping the vow of gratitude would make it to God's ears. "Now, could you help me figure out how to get Cache back? Bluebell here isn't helping."

By the time Wendy called, Karla had been back in her cabin for a couple of hours. Adele had gotten everyone to clear out, and she'd left the kindest note for Karla about how she was right next door and she'd be back later to check on her.

"Hey," she said to her sister, definitely more upbeat now than she'd been in the pasture. "How's work?"

"Horrible," Wendy said. "And Joey's been crying since I got home." She sounded miserable and tired, and Karla didn't want to burden her with more.

"I'm so sorry," she said. "Maybe you should quit."

"You know what? Jerome said the same thing. I think he was just trying to make me feel better."

"Well, your husband has a good job. You don't really have to go to work. Do you?" Karla once again thought of the iceberg. She only saw what Wendy wanted her to.

"I'm going to look at our budget," she said. "I've only been back to work for a week, and it's so hard. So much harder than I thought it would be." Scuffling came through the line, and she heard her whisper to her husband, "Thanks. Yes, I'll take him."

Karla wanted with everything inside her to be there for her sister, and she wondered if she could get in her car and leave the ranch as easily as Cache had.

"So what's up?" Wendy asked.

"Nothing," Karla said a little too quickly. "I was just thinking of booking my ticket soon." She sighed, hating the little fib though it didn't really hurt anyone. "And Cache broke up with me."

Surprisingly, she delivered the words without any catch in her voice.

"Oh, Karla, I'm sorry. What happened?"

She pressed her lips together as the emotion overcame her now. She shook her head, though Wendy wasn't there to see it.

"Karla, just...you like him right?"

"Yes," she said in a burst, thinking Wendy had gotten the wrong L-word.

"Then go fix it." She drew in a deep breath. "I know you don't want me to tell you that, but you called me. You didn't have to call me. If you like this man, and you want to be with him, then go fix it. You didn't even try to fix things with Jackson, and you've been miserable ever since. I'm sorry. I know you don't think you have. But you have."

Wendy blew out her breath and a soft baby noise came through the line. "At least until you started dating Cache. Now, I can see the happiness in your texts. It's almost infectious, even from all the way across the country."

Karla half-cried and half-laughed. "Okay," she said. "I'll go fix it. But Wendy, he's not even here anymore."

"Then go where he is. Don't wait. Remember how you didn't wait to go after your education or your career? When you're being proactive, you're happier."

Karla did know where Cache had gone. Maybe she didn't know the exact location of Shiloh Ridge, but she had a computer with the Internet. She knew how to drive. She knew how to use the GPS on her phone.

Standing, she turned in a circle as if some magical fairies would appear and help her start packing. She needed to talk to Scarlett, and Sissy, and Dave maybe about the cow cuddling. Or maybe she could just cancel. Someone else could water them.

Right?

"Are you even listening to me?" Wendy asked.

"Sorry," Karla said. "I got excited about making a plan and doing something."

Her sister laughed. "All right. Go do it. Text me the details—but not too late and not too early. I'm off tomorrow, thank the heavens."

Karla said, "Thank you so much, Wendy. I'm going to make this right."

"I know you will. Love you."

"Love you too, sis." She hung up and just stood in her living room, her brain throwing ideas at her like curve balls. "Scarlett," she said. "I have to start with Scarlett."

She left the cabin through the front door, not bothering to text Scarlett first to figure out where she was. If she wasn't at the homestead, then she'd do that. After knocking on the back door, her heart started pounding in her chest.

Worries started assaulting her. She couldn't leave the ranch. Or California. Both had become sanctuaries for her, and—Scarlett pulled open the door.

"Karla, thank the stars." She pulled Karla into a tight hug and added, "What happened? Cache left?" She stepped back and held Karla at arm's length. "He went to Shiloh Ridge."

"I know," Karla said. "I haven't heard from him or anything, so I don't know when he'll be back." With an awful feeling in her stomach, she realized he might never come back. "He'll come back, right?"

"He told Dave he'd be back in time for the wedding," Scarlett said, gesturing for Karla to come inside. "It's so hot out there. Get in here so we can keep the air conditioning inside."

Karla stepped into the homestead at the same time her phone chimed. She glanced at it, her pulse shooting toward the stars. "It's Cache." She swiped and tapped, the anticipation building to astronomical proportions in the three seconds it took for his message to appear on the screen.

Her hopes fell. "He just wants me to take care of the cattle and run cow cuddling."

"Hmm," Scarlett said, heading into the kitchen. "Tea?"

"It's a million degrees outside."

"Chocolate milk then." She stepped over to the fridge, and sure enough, she pulled out a gallon of chocolate milk. "I hate the stuff, but Hudson loves it." She smiled at Karla. "We won't tell him you had some. Besides, this situation calls for a lot of chocolate." She reached for her phone. "And we better get Adele over here."

"Scarlett," Karla said. "I want to go to Shiloh Ridge too."

The ranch owner smiled like she'd just gotten the greatest gift of her life, her fingers still flying over her screen as she texted Adele.

"Should I?" Karla asked, her familiar doubts rearing their ugly heads. "I mean, I know you need—"

"You should go," Scarlett said, finally looking up from her phone. "If you feel like you should go, you should go."

"What do I say to him?" she asked, and Scarlett turned to get down a couple of glasses.

"I can't tell you that, but Adele is on her way over, and I'm sure she'll have some opinions for you." Scarlett laughed, and Karla was suddenly very, very thankful for her girlfriends on this ranch—the very ones she was worried would judge her and Cache's relationship.

"You didn't start without me, did you?" Adele called as she entered the house. "I brought cookies." She appeared with a plate full of treats and concern on her face. After handing the cookies to Scarlett, she hugged Karla and said, "Okay, we need a strategy for Shiloh Ridge...."

Chapter Twenty-One

C ache stayed in bed as long as he was able, which meant he was up and in the kitchen with his father by six o'clock in the morning.

"Breakfast?" his dad asked, already pulling open the fridge. "Leo's bringing over some muffins we had on the ranch yesterday."

Cache's stomach seized at the idea of food. And at seeing Leo. He didn't want to eat, and he didn't want to talk.

"Brenda is great, Dad," he said, and his father turned toward him with a smile on his mouth but apprehension in his eyes.

"Yeah? You liked her?"

"A whole lot," Cache said, lifting his coffee mug to his lips. "Are you going to marry her?"

"I've been thinkin' about it," his dad said, cracking

open an egg in each hand and letting it drop into a bowl. "She don't want to live out on the ranch though, and it's a twenty-minute drive."

"Maybe you should retire," he said, and Leo entered the cabin through the back door just as Cache started the sentence.

"That's what I told him," Leo said, setting a box of muffins down on the counter. "He doesn't listen to me."

Cache wanted to scoff. His familiar feelings of never measuring up to Leo boiled to the surface no matter how he tried to cool them. He just looked at his brother and stirred his coffee.

"Did you talk to Karla?" Leo asked, apparently oblivious to the vibes coming off of Cache. He got down his own mug and poured himself some coffee while their dad put a frying pan on the stove and got the flame going under it.

"A little," Cache said.

"Then why are you here?" Leo asked.

"Because I broke up with her."

Leo rolled his eyes. "Come on."

"You shouldn't have been talking to her without me knowing," Cache said.

"We're not fifteen anymore," Leo said. "She wanted to have the perfect birthday party for you. *Perfect*, she said. I don't know why it mattered to her so much, but it did." He dumped too much sugar in his coffee and sat down at the table.

Cache wanted to leave, and he realized now why he'd gone to California while his father and brother had come to Texas. He loved his brother. He honestly did. But he didn't want to compete with him anymore. Their relationship had improved drastically over the past two years they'd lived on separate ranches, and Cache had only now realized it.

"Eggs," his dad said, setting the pan between them. Cache felt like he'd been transported to the past, where he and Leo sat at the kitchen table on the dairy farm, arguing about something. Whether a cow needed to be put down. Or sold. Or the price at which they were willing to sell their milk.

There was always something—even women, from time to time.

And their dad had always cooked while they talked, set food in front of them, and then joined them, giving the advice they were both too stubborn to see.

He didn't like this version of himself and didn't like that he felt trapped in this situation from the past.

This morning, though, his father sat down and dished himself some eggs without saying anything. Even Leo looked at him like he'd sprouted a second head. Cache and Leo exchanged a glance, still waiting for the advice to drop.

"I think I will ask Brenda to marry me," their dad said, glancing up from his breakfast. "Why aren't you eating?"

"Aren't you going to tell Cache what to do?" Leo

asked. "Or me?" He picked up the bowl of scrambled eggs, but he simply held it without putting any on his plate.

"Nope," his dad said, and Cache didn't like this break in the routine. Or maybe he did. He wasn't sure. "But you better eat and then get on to your chores. Bear won't tolerate any slack today, not after the week we've had."

Cache had kept up with the wolf attacks on the cattle here at Shiloh Ridge. He got along fine with Leo through texts, and when he didn't have to coordinate with him to make decisions.

"I can help," Cache said, picking up his fork and taking the bowl of eggs from Leo.

"You should go back to California," Leo said.

His dad shook his head. "No, he should go out to the front porch."

Cache put eggs on his plate, more confusion cutting through him than he could think through. "The porch?" he and Leo said at the same time.

Leo beat him to the punch—just like always—and he strode across the cabin to the front window. Cache had started to get up, but he settled back into his chair. Let Leo take care of it. Leo always did.

Perfect, wonderful, handsome Leo.

Cache didn't like the poisonous thoughts in his mind, and they made the eggs taste bad too.

"Cache," his dad said, leaning forward like his voice wouldn't echo through the whole house. Behind them, Leo said something, but Cache didn't hear him. His father wore so much earnestness in his expression that it completely captivated Cache.

"What, Dad?"

"Forget about Leo. He didn't do anything wrong, and neither did Karla."

Cache sucked in a breath. "Dad." He shook his head, his thoughts tumbling with the motion.

"Trust me, son." He leaned back. "Go eat your eggs out on the porch." He dug back into his breakfast, the advice portion of the day obviously over.

Cache still hesitated, especially when Leo returned to the table and said, "There's nothing out there, Dad."

His dad lifted one shoulder in a shrug. "All right." He looked at Cache and put the last bite of eggs in his mouth. "I'm out to the fences this morning. I'll see you two at dinner."

Ranching took all day, and the job was never done. Cache's father loved it, though, and Cache always had too. He admired his dad for his work ethic, and he'd learned so much from him.

He got to his feet and joined his dad at the kitchen sink. "Thanks for letting me crash here, Dad." He hugged his father. "Be careful out on the fences."

"I will. Love you, son." He took his hat from the peg by the back door and left Cache and Leo alone.

Cache really didn't want to talk about Karla with his brother, so he stopped by the table to grab his coffee, and then he went out onto the front porch like his dad had suggested. A rocking chair sat there, along with a small side table, perfect for holding mugs of coffee for a cowboy.

He sighed as he settled into the rocking chair. "Could I move here?" he wondered aloud, but the feelings that overcame him felt like a dark storm. No, he would not be moving to Shiloh Ridge.

Carson had come here after he and Adele had split up, and he'd liked it. But Carson's older brother wasn't here, with his perpetually long shadow and annoying habits of sticking his nose where it didn't belong.

Cache closed his eyes and prayed, hoping a solution would come forward in his mind. Karla had never responded to his text about taking care of the cows or canceling the cow cuddling sessions Cache would miss, and he didn't like that.

He wasn't the type to leave his responsibilities unattended. But he wasn't going to text her again. He also wasn't the groveling type or the unkind type, though he had said something very mean to her before he'd left

"Maybe I should apologize for that...." he muttered to himself. He pulled out his phone and looked at it at the same time the distinct sound of a car approaching the cabin entered his ears. His father lived down at the end of the lane, in a cabin surrounded almost entirely by pine trees, and no one had much of a reason to come down here.

But someone was definitely coming. Cache had heard the tell-tale sound of tires on gravel enough to know.

Sure enough, a gray sedan poked through the trees, easing to a stop with several yards to go.

Cache peered at the driver, but he couldn't see through the glare on the front windshield. He wasn't sure they could see him up on the porch either, as the eaves on the cabins here were low and thick, great for keeping the snow on the roof instead of falling to the ground.

Karla got out of the car.

Cache's heart stopped.

She looked left and right and down at her phone before focusing on the cabin again. So she definitely couldn't see him, and part of him wished he could rock backward and right through the wall so he could run out the back door and avoid her.

At the same time, nothing in him wanted to avoid her.

He found himself standing. Their eyes met, and Karla lifted one hand in a half-hearted wave. She didn't smile, and she didn't take a step. She wore jeans that might as well have been painted on, with a mustard yellow blouse with flowers all over it.

Her hair was stunning as it flowed over her shoulders and with those cowgirl boots on, Cache's blood started heating and pumping and zipping through his body.

Karla was here.

Karla wasn't going to let him walk out of her life.

For some reason, that made Cache happier than he'd thought it would, and he moved to the top of the steps.

Then down them. He paused there and blinked. Yep, she was still there.

"Do you have a couple of minutes to talk?" she asked, her voice getting swallowed by the huge Texas sky and all the trees surrounding them.

He nodded, because he couldn't seem to get his voice to work. Karla moved then, coming closer and closer to him. When she stood only a few feet away, she stalled and looked up at him, neither one of them saying a word.

Chapter Twenty-Two

Karla's pulse took all of her concentration. All of her body's brain power. She'd made it to Shiloh Ridge, and Cache was standing right in front of her.

"Are you going to say anything?" he asked.

Karla had never said a whole lot. She showed. Her coming all this way should mean something to him, and by the way he gazed at her with that soft glint in his eye, it did.

"I didn't want to wait for you to come back on Sunday," she said. "I asked Scarlett to take care of the cows, and she said she would."

He nodded, glancing to his right where something crunched in the woods. Karla didn't like all the trees, how closed in this ranch felt. She took another step toward Cache.

"I know you said you didn't love me, and that's fine.

Really, it is." She pressed her fingertips together, trying to get both sides of her brain to cooperate with one another. "I wanted you to know how I feel about you, because I don't always say it in words."

"You're here," he said while she took a breath to continue.

The air stuck in her lungs. "Yeah," she said, her next sentence flying out of her brain. "I'm here."

"Karla." He reached out and brushed his fingers along hers. "I know you do things to show how you feel. I know that." He ducked his head, concealing his eyes from her. "I said some mean things. Things I didn't mean."

Karla's stomach quaked, the memory of those words so fresh and so cutting.

"I'm sorry." He lifted his eyes to hers. "I just...Leo is a trigger for me, and I thought you knew that."

Karla did know that, but she couldn't get her voice to work. She'd cried enough since he'd left yesterday, and if Adele hadn't been with her at the airport, she'd probably be sitting in her cabin at Last Chance Ranch instead of here in front of him.

"Hey, don't cry," he said, wiping her calloused hand across her cheek.

Karla sniffed and stepped back. She didn't even know she'd started crying. Wiping at her eyes, she said, "I like being your girlfriend. I liked it when we were secret, but I like it when we're not too."

His mouth curved slightly. "I sense a but."

"No buts," she said. "I'm also not going to keep any more secrets from you. No surprises. Nothing." She just wanted him to come back. She hadn't even realized how big of a piece of her heart he'd claimed until he wasn't there. She felt hollow without him, without his gentle influence in her life, without the peace he'd brought her by not judging her for her past.

"I like surprises," he said. "Just not secrets."

"Well, you blew the party," she said, feeling more normal. A laugh burst out of her mouth, but more tears streamed down her face. "I'm so sorry, Cache," she said, her voice choked and too high.

"It's okay." He gathered her into his strong embrace and held her close. She seized onto that peace, that forgiveness he always so freely gave. "I don't think you cheated on me with Leo," he said softly. "But that's how I felt. I sort of went crazy. I just...I don't think you'll do that. Honest, I don't."

Karla nodded against his chest. "I love you."

"And I love you." He put a few inches between them but kept his hands on her waist. His hat bumped her forehead, and she reached up and took it off. He kissed her then, and Karla had never been happier that she'd left California.

He didn't kiss her long, and Karla laid her cheek against his chest. "I want to take you home to meet my family," she whispered.

"Yeah?" he asked. "No secrets with them?"

"No." She stepped out of his arms and pulled her phone from her pocket. "And I want you to read the texts I sent to Leo."

"Karla, I don't need to do that."

"But *I* need you to do it," she said. "I didn't delete a single one, and I did talk to him on the phone twice, but I swear we just talked about you." She shook her phone at him when he wouldn't take it.

He wore a look of doubt on his face, but he finally took her device. His hand fell to his side. "I don't care what you said to him. I—"

"I know you, Cache," she interrupted. "You do care, number one. And number two, Leo didn't tell me anything I didn't already know." She pressed one palm to his heart. "I do know you." She backed up a step, then another. "I'm going to go get breakfast, and I'll be back in a little bit." With that, she turned and walked back to the rental car.

Cache still stood there on the gravel in front of his father's cabin when she backed up. But he was looking at her phone, that cowboy hat hiding his expression from her.

Didn't matter. Karla knew he needed to see the texts, and she was glad she'd insisted he look at them. She knew what secret communication did to people—it had ruined her marriage. She should've known better than to open the channels of communication between her and Leo. Maybe she was naïve to think Cache wouldn't mind.

He had told her that story about his brother, but she hadn't internalized it enough.

"Obviously," she told herself as she drove the narrow roads back to the epicenter of the ranch. When her tires finally met asphalt, relief spread through her. Texas was beautiful, and the town of Shiloh Ridge felt like something out of a Christmas postcard. Even in August, there were wreaths on the lampposts and a huge Christmas tree next to an old, red-brick building in the center of town.

Right next to that, the diner Carson had told her about had a line of people waiting outside it. Carson had told her she'd be tempted to go somewhere else, and she should resist that. So she parked down the street a little ways and walked back to join the line.

It had moved inside now, and Carson was right. Things moved quickly there, and she didn't need a table anyway. Once through the door, she spotted the to-go line and stepped over to it.

She felt a little out of sorts without her phone to keep her occupied. Glancing around the diner, she found the place lively and vibrant, full of the scent of bacon, cowboys, and hot coffee. She wanted all three, and she smiled to herself at the very idea of making a lasting relationship with Cache.

They hadn't talked about marriage yet, though he had said early on in their relationship he wasn't worried about her cheating on him because they'd love each other so deeply.

Please let that be true, she prayed.

When it was her turn to order, she got bacon and egg

plates for her and Cache, substituting a pancake in hers and adding salsa to his.

She wanted to call her sister and tell her she'd fixed the problem with Cache. At least she hoped she had. He'd kissed her like she had. She wanted to meet his family too —no secrets.

Back at the ranch, she pulled further into the driveway and found Cache sitting on the top step. He met her at the door and took the food with a quick smile. She followed him into the cabin, which held more charm than the ones at Last Chance Ranch. It was almost like everything in Shiloh Ridge, including the ranch, had been touched by magic.

Even Karla felt different here. "So," she said as she sat down and opened her container of food. "We're okay, right?"

He placed her phone on the table in front of her. "We're okay."

She smiled at him and picked up her fork. "Good. Because I don't think I could've eaten this pancake if we weren't."

He chuckled and spread his salsa over his eggs. "I did want to talk to you about something."

"Yeah?"

"Yeah." He put a bite of eggs in his mouth and chewed, prolonging the conversation. He swallowed and said, "Marriage. Me and you. What are your thoughts on that?"

Warmth spread through Karla, making every cell tingle. "I think that's a great idea."

"Tell me what you're envisioning," he said. "You've been married before. Was it big? What time of year?"

Karla told him all about the fall wedding in Virginia and how she'd been engaged for over a year. "We don't need to do anything like that," she said.

"No?"

"I think Lisa will kill me if I get married before her and steal our mother's attention. But maybe just after that. I can coordinate it all and just invite my family." She poured maple syrup from the cutest little bottle over her pancake. "Will your family come to the ranch?"

"You want to get married on the ranch?" His eyebrows went up, matching the surprise in his voice.

She blinked at him. "Yes."

He nodded. "My dad's probably going to get married soon. I asked him and Leo to come back for lunch so they could meet you. I don't know how long you're planning to stay."

"I don't actually have a ticket back to California yet," she said. "I wasn't sure if you'd talk to me, or how long I'd be here."

Something like regret touched his eyes. "I'm sorry, Karla. I—didn't mean to make you do something you didn't want to do. I didn't mean to push you away."

"You didn't," she said. "I'm really great at doing those

things myself." She managed a weak smile, but Cache didn't return it.

"One more serious question," he said. "And then we can go meet the cows."

"The cows?"

"Yeah, I have hundreds of cows here. Well, I mean, Leo and my dad do."

And cows were important to Cache, so Karla nodded. "Yeah, I want to meet them."

And she thought she knew what he was going to ask next, so she wasn't surprised when he said, "Do you want kids, Karla?"

"Yeah," she said, the last of the sadness over her miscarriage years ago finally fading. "I do want kids, Cache. *Your* kids." She honestly wasn't sure if she could have kids with her history and her age, but she did want them.

Cache finally grinned that full-wattage grin she'd seen on his face so often. "Great," he said. "Me too."

WHEN THEY WALKED into the cabin for lunch, two other men were already there. His brother and his father, obviously. Karla could see Cache in both of them, and she knew instantly that his bright blue eyes must have come from his mother.

His father had dark eyes that saw everything about her

in two seconds flat. And he liked her instantly, she could tell. "You must be Karla." He hugged her quickly and added, "The pizza is almost done."

"My dad, Woody."

"Nice to meet you." Karla wasn't hungry at all, but she'd eat to be nice. She looked at Leo, who bore more of a resemblance to his father than to Cache. Everything was just washed out a bit. His hair sat somewhere between the two of them, and his eyes seemed more gray than blue or brown.

"Hello, Leo," she said, regretting the formality.

Cache laughed and nudged her toward him. "My older brother," he said. "Leo, this is Karla."

"Just as pretty as she sounds," Leo said with a smile, and Karla couldn't decide if he was flirting or just being kind.

She shook his hand and retreated to Cache's side. No one said anything, and these Bryant men didn't seem to mind the silence. It drove Karla toward battiness, and thankfully, the timer on the oven went off and activity ensued.

Leo got down plates while his father pulled out the pizza and cut it. When they'd all crowded around the table, Woody said, "I think I'm going to ask Brenda to marry me today."

Cache choked and Leo dropped his piece of pizza with a wet thud. "Today?" he asked while Cache coughed.

Karla picked up a can of lemonade and opened it for

him. "That's great," she said. "How are you going to propose?"

"I think I'll just show up at her house and ask her," Woody said, looking around at everyone.

Cache quieted and said, "Good idea, Dad," and Karla picked up her phone to send him a quick text. *I want more of a proposal than that. Please don't just show up at my house and ask me.*

His phone lit up, and he glanced at it. A swipe and a tap later, their eyes met. Karla nodded and Cache smiled, and everything seemed absolutely right in the world.

Finally.

Chapter Twenty-Three

C ache tugged at the tie around his neck, wishing Dave had chosen a normal tie for his groomsmen. Of course, Cache knew Dave hadn't really chosen anything for the wedding, so he should be blaming Sissy for the agonizingly tight bowtie currently cutting off his air supply.

He'd been back in town for a couple of days, and life had gone on as normal on the ranch. Karla hadn't stayed long in Shiloh Ridge, but Cache had hung around while his father proposed to Brenda. They'd had a big dinner celebration at the ranch, where Cache had met the owner, Bear Glover. And then a smaller shindig at his dad's cabin the night before he'd left.

He liked the air much better in California, and it was all because it was the same oxygen Karla breathed.

Sissy had paired him with her to walk down the aisle,

and Cache's nerves seemed to be rioting about it for some reason. Almost like it was their wedding—or at least a preview of it. And he knew neither of them were really ready to get married, though they'd talked about all of those serious things in Texas.

It wasn't until he and Karla had been able to cuddle into Cookie's side that Cache felt secure in his relationship with her. She'd been madly baking to make sure Dave and Sissy's wedding cake would be perfect, and she wouldn't let anyone see it. Not even the bride.

Someone knocked on his front door, and he turned away from the view out his back window, his mind switching from where he and Karla would live once they tied the knot to putting on a smile and mustering up all the support he could for one of his best friends.

"Ready?" Lance asked on the other side of the door, and Cache nodded as he stepped onto the porch with him.

"Why is your tie like that?" Cache asked, glaring at Lance's tie. It didn't seem to have a pythonic grip around his throat.

Lance chuckled, but that only made Cache's mood darken. "Fix mine," he said, and Lance started tugging and twisting to get the tie right. It finally loosened, and a sense of relief cascaded through Cache. "Thanks."

Lance stepped back, turning serious as he surveyed Cache in his more formal attire. "The boots look good," he said.

"Thanks," Cache said, glancing down at them. "My

dad bought them for me. An early birthday present. I have to wear them to his wedding too."

"And church," Lance said. "I like my dress boots for that."

Cache had honestly never bothered with dress cowboy boots, but he did like the black pair he wore right now a whole lot. He and Lance went down the steps together and started over toward the administration building where Sissy had chosen to set up their wedding.

Sweat ran down his face before they reached the turn in the road, and he started thinking he and Karla should opt for a winter wedding date. *Maybe February*, he thought.

The admin building was air conditioned, and Cache found Dave in a room with a few other cowboys and his dad. He knew enough to stay out of the way and do what he was told, which was exactly what he did until an intercom beeped and a woman said, "Dave, can you send your party out to line up? And then take your spot, please."

"All right, guys," Dave said. "You heard her."

Cache didn't know who she was, but he stepped over to Dave and gave him a quick embrace with a man-clap on the shoulder. "Good luck, man," he said before following the others out the door and down the hall.

Sissy had a huge bridal party, and the space under the shade of the tent where she and Dave would be married was already taken by the time Cache got there.

"Hey," Karla said, appearing at his side.

"Hey." A smile moved through his whole body at the sight of her. "You look beautiful."

She glanced around as if someone might pop out of thin air and contradict him. "When we get married, we are not having any bridesmaids," she muttered. She linked her arm through his and tugged him to the left and into a part of the shade that hadn't been claimed yet.

"No?" he asked, grinning down at her. "Why not?"

"I hate these dresses." She looked as put out as he'd been about the choking tie. "At least Sissy has normal colors." Karla shook her head. "No, I just want something simple for our wedding. People should just show up after work one day and then I'll feed them."

Cache almost scoffed. Thankfully, he sucked it in when he realized she was serious. "Really?" he asked.

She shrugged. "I mean, I've been married before. I don't need a whole show."

Cache laced his fingers between hers. "What if I want the whole show?"

She looked at him, surprise in her eyes. "Do you?"

He enjoyed going against something she thought she knew about him, and he shrugged casually to prolong the moment. "Not really. I would like the cows there."

Karla laughed, earning her a few glares from nearby patrons. She took the volume down and covered her mouth, her eyes still crinkled. "Of course. You and the cows."

"Hey, you like those cows too."

"Yeah, but they can't be bridesmaids."

"Why not? I bet you could put skirts on them. Tutus."

Karla dissolved into another round of giggles, and one of the older people nearby actually shushed her.

"The wedding hasn't even started yet," Karla said.

"Dave's up front," Cache said, peering over the tops of the chairs. "We should probably line up." He moved over to the rest of the group, and everyone fell into line.

It seemed like a really long time, and he leaned over to Karla and said, "Please don't take this long while I'm standing up there. Look at him. Dave looks like he's about to pass out."

Karla tightened her grip on Cache's arm, and said, "Deal. I'll give you thirty seconds to get in place and no more." She beamed up at him, and a strong feeling of love moved through him.

"I love you," he whispered, scanning that pale pink dress again as it hugged her curves and fell to her ankles. "Tall heels?"

"Yes, so hold onto me," she said. "I don't want to trip."

A MONTH LATER, the weather started to cool. A month after that, Cache and the band played at the Pasadena Halloween festival, which they'd done in years past. With

Sawyer and Dave married now, Cache had expected the band to slow down. Maybe even break up.

But they hadn't, though Cache had relaxed quite a lot. After all, a lot of his energy needed to go to Karla these days, just like Sawyer's went to Jeri and his new son, and Dave's went to Sissy and the adoption process they were starting.

He'd been thinking a lot about asking Karla to marry him, but he didn't have a ring and they'd never really talked about it again.

She didn't act like she minded all that much. He still found her in the pasture every day, and they still snuck kisses from the safety of the cow cuddling barrier. They ran the cuddling classes, and life was going well.

Karla burst into his house one morning while he stood in the kitchen, a fresh mug of coffee in his hand. He dropped it, and the shattering sound of breaking glass mingled with the hot splash of coffee everywhere.

"Oh, no," she said, "I'm so sorry. I was just so excited, and I figured it would be okay if I came in." She crossed through the cabin to him, while he stood there and stared at the mess.

"It's fine," he said, finally reaching for a wash cloth. "What are we excited about?"

"The trip."

The coffee wiped up easily as she picked out the bigger pieces of the mug. "The trip to Virginia?" he asked.

"Yeah," she said.

"When's that again?" he asked. She was supposed to go in August, but something had happened with her sister's dress, and she'd asked Karla to delay the trip.

"You're kidding, right?" Karla stilled and looked at him. He kept mopping up the coffee. "Cache."

"My bag's right there," he said. "Now, if someone hadn't made me drop this mug, we'd be on our way to the airport." And when they finished flying all the way across the country, he'd meet her family.

He wasn't sure why the thought made his nerves quake, only that it did. She'd told them about him. They knew what he did for a living, and she's assured him he didn't have to be anyone but himself.

"I've already broken my father's heart," she'd said. "You're a huge step from Jackson."

Cache had never met Jackson, so he couldn't be sure. But yeah, he wasn't taking Karla from her family and flying across the country. She was already here.

With the mess cleaned up, he poured himself another mug and offered her one. "No, I want that mocha from Beans and Brew."

"Well, we better go then," he said. "If we have to make a stop."

"We have plenty of time."

"Have you driven in LA traffic?" He gave her a raised-eyebrow look and went to get his bag. "I wanted to ask you something we haven't quite talked about yet."

"Oh yeah?" She pulled the door closed behind them

and came down the steps while he loaded his luggage in the back seat of her car with hers.

"Yeah." He paused and looked at her. Lifted his coffee to take a sip as he peered over the rim of the mug. "Where we'll live when we get married."

They hadn't talked about anything like this since Dave and Sissy's wedding, and the shock in Karla's eyes testified of that.

"I'm thinking your cabin," he said. "Do you pay Scarlett rent?"

"No," she said, her eyes searching his, looking for an answer.

Cache wasn't sure what it would be. Yes, he and Karla would still be working for the ranch, so maybe they could just share the cabin on the back lawn of the homestead without a problem. "Maybe we should talk to her about it when we get back."

"Maybe you should ask me to marry you first," she said, almost rolling her eyes as she turned toward the passenger door and opened it.

"Maybe you should tell me what kind of ring you want."

She froze for the second time that morning and asked, "Really?"

"It's a long drive, sweetheart. Start talking."

Chapter Twenty-Four

Karla didn't need Cache to buy her a diamond ring. She had the perfect one back in Virginia—which was the real reason for her excitement to be flying across the country. Sure, she wanted to introduce Cache to her parents and her sisters. She wanted to hold her baby nephew and smell the powdery scent of his hair. She wanted to help Lisa with her wedding plans, which included the bridesmaids dresses.

She'd spoken true when she'd said she didn't want a big wedding. Or the ugly, uncomfortable bridesmaids dresses every bride seemed to have. Heck, she'd had them the first time too.

But this time...this time, she wanted the men in jeans and checkered shirts, and women in denim skirts, and everyone to be wearing cowboy boots while she and Cache said I do near the water pump in the cow pasture.

If the man would ask her to marry him, that was.

Doesn't matter, she told herself as he pulled up to the drive-through at Beans and Brew and ordered her mocha. *You can ask him when you get to Virginia.*

Her mother had confirmed that her great-grandmother's ring was still available, and that Karla could absolutely have it if she wanted it.

She turned the conversation toward something else on the sluggish drive through city traffic, and after that, Cache turned quiet. She supposed meeting her family was a big deal, but at least he wasn't showing up at her dad's house, hoping she'd talk to him.

Now *that* had been hard.

She slept most of the way across the country, and it was dark by the time the plane landed in Norfolk. They'd packed light, so they didn't have baggage to wait for, and Karla led him out onto the street to the pickup area.

After her mom picked up her call, Karla said, "We're at pickup eight."

"Almost there," her mom said, and Karla shivered in the chilly air. She hung up and nestled into Cache's chest.

"See why I don't want to live here? It's freezing."

"It's not terrible," he said. "It's just the wind."

It was windy, and thankfully, her father pulled up to the curb in their sensible sedan a few moments later. He and her mother got out of the car, and Karla squeezed Cache's hand. He looked like someone had petrified him, and she prayed this would go well. She had no reason to think it wouldn't.

"Mom," she said, tears pricking her eyes. She did miss her mom a lot. She dropped Cache's hand to hug her mom, and she held on extra tight for only a heartbeat. "So this is Cache Bryant, my boyfriend." She beamed up at him and then quickly shifted her gaze to her dad's face so she could judge his reaction.

He smiled, but it felt a little forced. "Cache, this is my dad, Deacon, and my mom, Denise."

"Nice to meet you, sir," Cache said, and he sounded so country western that Karla burst out laughing.

"What?" her mom asked, looking back and forth between them.

"Nothing," Karla said, still giggling a little.

"Ma'am." Cache tipped his hat at her mother and accepted the hug.

"Who's hungry?" her mom asked, still glancing at Cache like he had something wrong with him.

"Starving," Karla said as her dad lifted their bags into the trunk. "Wasn't Wendy making dinner?"

"Yes," her mother said. "We'll just go to her place if you're ready."

"Ready," Cache and Karla said at the same time, and a rush of happiness hit her.

In the back seat, she texted Lisa, *Are we ready?*

It's on, her sister's message came back, and Karla glanced at Cache to make sure he wasn't watching.

He had his head leaned against the window, his eyes closed. She felt such love for him in that moment that her breath caught, and she sure hoped he wouldn't be upset when she proposed to him.

"THAT WAS SO GOOD," Cache said an hour later, and Wendy's smile could've lit New York City.

"I'm glad you enjoyed it," she said, turning toward Joey as the baby fussed.

"We should go," her mom said, and Karla's muscles seized. Lisa had been giving her a *are you going to do it now?* look for the past thirty minutes, but Karla hadn't been able to get up and get the job done.

And now they were leaving.

"It's fine, Mom," Wendy said. "I'm not working anymore, remember?"

"I know, but Joey's tired."

Among all the hustle and bustle of putting on jackets and clearing dishes, Karla snuck into the living room with Lisa, who handed her a plastic zipper bag with the ring it. Not exactly romantic, but the box was long gone.

"Hurry up," she said. "He's perfect for you Karla, and you're going to miss your chance."

"You think he's perfect for me?"

"Are you kidding? He's gorgeous, employed, and the

kindest man I've ever met. He obviously adores you. Now, get in there and ask him to marry you." Lisa gave her a little shove, and Karla took a long, deep breath, hoping this didn't backfire.

Around the corner, her eyes landed first on Cache, who'd obviously been looking for her. "There you are," he said, and that somehow stopped the other conversations.

"I had to get something," she said, her heartbeat quaking as much now as it had in that forest in Texas. She didn't allow herself to fall into a staring trance now as she had then, but instead took a step toward him.

She held up the ring, pinched precariously between her thumb and forefinger. "I am in love with you," she said. "I want to get married on the ranch, with all the cows in tutus, and you in those fancy dress boots you love, and that blue shirt you won't throw away."

His eyes widened, and he simply stared at her. She glanced at her mother, who had one hand over her heart as tears streamed down her face. Her dad put his arm around her, and Karla wanted that level of love and tenderness in her life too. Now, in ten years, and then twenty, and then forty, when she and Cache were old and gray.

"This is my great-grandmother's ring. I want to wear it while we're engaged, and then we can pick out another one together." She handed it to him, and he stared at it as it rested in his palm.

"Cache Bryant, will you marry me?"

He brought his eyes back to hers, so many emotions swimming in them she couldn't decipher them all. Definitely love. Surprise. Heat. Desire.

"Yes," he said simply, and the room erupted in cheers. She laughed and cupped his face in both of her hands as they kissed, and her hand shook as he slid the heirloom on her finger. Congratulations went around, and hugging, and Joey cried and cried, and finally, they all went out the front door.

Karla let everyone go ahead of them, tugging on Cache's hand to get him to stay on the front porch of her sister's house with her.

"You're not mad? That was okay?"

"Not mad," he said, leaning down and touching the tip of his nose to hers. "I'd love to pick a ring out for you together later."

"I love you," she whispered, her lips catching on his as she pressed into him.

"I don't think that blue shirt is appropriate for a wedding," he whispered back, a chuckle rumbling through his chest.

"Mm." She let her eyes drift closed, waiting for him to kiss her.

"But I will wear the boots." He touched his lips to hers in a gentle kiss. "I love you, Karla."

"And it's not a secret that I love you, too."

Read on for a sneak peek at **LAST CHANCE CHRISTMAS**, the final book in this series!

Sneak Peek! Last Chance Christmas - Chapter One

L ance Longcomb bent to get another brick, the
  wicked January wind threatening to unseat his
cowboy hat. He mashed it on his head, actually grateful
for it. Laying brick was no joke, and though the weather
had threatened rain today, so far, only the sky foamed with
angry clouds. No moisture yet.

He'd cover the new entrance gate to the ranch once it
did, but it wouldn't be the end of his workday. Lance spent
long hours in the Canine Club and out with the horses
when he wasn't doing specific tasks Hudson assigned him.

Working kept him busy. Kept his thoughts from going
around and around in circles. Kept him from reminding
himself that the only woman he'd had eyes for in the past
two years had yet another boyfriend.

Not only that, but Amber was dating another cowboy
on the ranch. Dave had told Lance to wait. Watch. She'd

break up with him eventually. And she had. But before Lance could ask her out, Ames had. That hadn't lasted long. And now she was seeing another volunteer, one who came out to the ranch several times a week.

"Gotta move on," Lance muttered to himself. Problem was, there was nowhere to move to, and no one else he even cared about. So he mixed cement and layered it on top of the row he'd already done. Put the bricks on. Moved the trowel.

Work, work, work.

And when he wasn't working, he spent time with his band, though they'd all now found women to love. Dave and Sawyer and Carson were all married now, and Cache and Karla would be before long.

Lance had honestly started spending more time with Ames and Gray, though the cowboy from down south annoyed Lance with his loud voice and general arrogance.

The engine of a truck met his ears, and Lance stood back off the road as Dave's big black truck rumbled by. He pulled to a stop next to Lance, who said, "Going to the base?"

"Yep." Dave looked at him and then the wall. "What are you doin' this weekend?"

"Same old," Lance said. And he was tired of it. Something in his life had to change, but he didn't know what. *Show me what to do, Lord*, he thought as Dave knocked on the side of his truck.

"See you Monday."

"Have a good one." Lance lifted one gloved hand in good-bye, wishing he was the one driving away from the ranch.

Even as he thought it, he knew it wasn't true. Last Chance Ranch had been a sanctuary to him the same way it was for the rescue animals so many labored to help and protect. He'd come to the ranch after a divorce that had left his heart broken and his soul filled with darkness.

With prayer and the new job, he'd managed to keep getting up in the morning. With the help of his family and his new cowboy friends, he'd managed to find a measure of joy again. He still felt somewhat empty inside, though every time he went to church, that lessened.

At least until he saw Amber again.

Then he was reminded of his insane attraction to her. Sure, she was beautiful, with long, gorgeous blonde hair Lance wanted nothing more than to fist in his fingers as he kissed her. But he'd been around pretty women before. Lots of them. He'd married one.

Why Amber affected him so strongly, he wasn't sure. Only that something had sparked the moment he'd laid eyes on her and hadn't stopped in the time they'd worked together, despite him going out with other women. Despite her flitting from one boyfriend to the next every few months.

He'd love to be with her for just a few months.

Thunder clapped in the clouds above, and Lance decided he'd set his last brick for the day. He hurried to pull the thick plastic over the section of the wall he'd been working on for a couple of hours. No reason to have to redo it later, and he really liked the red brick Hudson and Scarlett had chosen for the gate flanking the dirt road up to the ranch.

They still had Prime, the robot mailbox that welcomed everyone to the ranch once they'd gone a half a mile down that dirt road. The wreath and tinsel that Prime had been holding for a month was gone now, and soon he'd have a big pink heart on his chest to celebrate Valentine's Day.

Lance was dreading the holiday, but he put it out of his mind as he stepped into the road, tugging on the plastic to get it into place.

A car turned off the main road at a speed that was much too fast for him to get out of the way. He froze, the same way deer did, he supposed.

The driver slammed on the brakes, and Lance managed to dance out of the way. The car swerved toward the wall he'd spent the last three hours building, and he thought that might be as bad as him getting hit by the vehicle.

"Wait, wait," he said as the car came to a stop. Frustration and annoyance surged within him, but he just stood there with one hand clutching the plastic that still wasn't in place. His heart pounded in his chest as the first raindrops fell.

The driver's door opened, and a woman jumped from the car. Not just any woman. Amber Haws.

"Lance," she said, her voice high-pitched, her face red, her eyes weeping. "I'm so sorry." She sobbed immediately afterward, and Lance had no idea what to do.

He looked at the wall, which she hadn't touched. With his eyes back on her, he had no idea what to do. "You didn't hit it," he said. She had a good three feet to go. He wondered if she'd have hit him, standing in the road.

She shook her head, angry little bursts of movement. The rain started to fall in earnest, and Lance was torn. He needed to cover the wall, but he had the woman of his dreams standing in front of him, crying.

"Amber," he said. "Get in the car, okay? Let me cover up this wall, and I'll come help you."

Thankfully, she did as he said, and he hastened to get the plastic in place. Facing the car, with his shoulders soaking wet, he started toward the passenger door. He opened it and slid in, a sigh slipping between his lips.

Her car smelled like his fantasies. Something floral, something peachy, and something so feminine the hole inside him widened, reminding him of how lonely he was.

"What's going on?" he asked easily, like maybe they'd go to lunch in a few minutes, and they were just catching up on small talk.

"What is with you cowboys?" she asked, her voice full of acid. She looked at him, the brown eyes that often followed him into sleep accusatory and full of sharpness.

"I'm sorry?"

"I'm so done with cowboys. Just done." She clenched

her fingers around the steering wheel. "Rude, ignorant, arrogant...." Her voice trailed off as she put her car in reverse and got it centered back on the road.

Lance had no idea what was going on, but he knew he didn't need a ride up to the ranch. "Hey, I have my truck," he said as she jammed her foot on the accelerator. He grunted and reached for the handle above the window as he got whiplashed backward.

Amber slammed on the brakes again, and Lance severely regretted getting in the car with her. He thought maybe he'd be able to help her, make her see that all that flirting six months ago had been real for him. That he wanted to touch her softly again, laugh with her, show her that not all cowboys were bad.

She skidded to a stop on the road beside where he'd left his truck. "There you go."

His chest heaved as if he'd just run a marathon, and adrenaline skipped through his bloodstream. He looked at her, the fire in her face scorching hot. "Amber," he said, but he didn't know how to finish it.

"Dwayne broke up with me," she said, the anger crumpling from her fine features. "On the *phone*, Lance. As he left town." Her breath hitched, and her voice broke, and those fingers strangled the steering wheel.

"I'm sorry," Lance said, though he secretly started rejoicing. If only she hadn't said *I'm so done with cowboys. Just done.*

As far as he'd known, Dwayne wasn't even a cowboy.

Sure, he might wear a hat when he came out to walk dogs, but that didn't make him a cowboy.

"I don't mean to be rude," she said. "But I'm late for work."

Time spun forward then, and Lance scrambled for the door handle. "Of course. I'm—I'll—sorry." He got out of the car and backed up as she floored the accelerator again. The tires spun on the slightly wet dirt, and when they found purchase, they kicked gravel out behind them.

Lance stood there as the sky opened up and drenched him, sure the woman had just driven away with his heart.

When his doorbell rang that night, Lance just glanced at it. It could only be one of three people, and Cache, Ames, or Gray would just walk in. Sure enough, the door opened a moment later, and Cache walked in, a couple of pizza boxes in his hand.

Ames entered behind him, and while Lance was happy for the food, he didn't really want the company. He'd been going over everything he and Amber had said to each other last July when they'd flirted at the animal adoption event.

That had been a great few hours and then a few days. But she'd started dating someone else, and Lance had faded into the background again.

But she had to know how much he liked her. Maybe

he should ask her out now. Not wait another moment. Another hour. Another day.

Sure, she'd almost hit him and then the wall he'd been building. She'd been crying and had basically sworn off men right in front of him. But someone else would ask her out, and she'd say yes. Lance just knew it.

Lance wanted to be the guy she said yes to.

"Supreme and Hawaiian," Cache said. "Karla's bringing dessert, if that's all right."

"I don't mean to keep you from her," Lance said, pushing himself off the couch. His whole body hurt, but he didn't let the groan come out of his mouth.

"She said she'd give us a twenty-minute head start," Cache said, moving into the kitchen and putting the pizza on the counter.

"Head start for what?" Lance asked.

"All the women have been with Amber all afternoon." Cache faced him, his eyes bright and shining and knowing. "Her boyfriend broke up with her. Now's your chance, man."

Lance opened his mouth to respond, but no words came. He scoffed and looked at Ames. "What's he talking about?"

"You're not going to let her get away again," Ames said. "We're not going to let you."

"Yeah," Cache said. "So we have twenty minutes to figure out your next move with Amber, or else Karla's going to tell you what to do."

Horror struck Lance right between the ribs. "I don't need all the women on this ranch gossiping about me," he said.

"It's not *all* the women," Cache said. "Just Karla, and only because I may have mentioned something about you and Amber."

"Cache," Lance said, exasperated with everything lately. He got out a stack of paper plates and opened the pizza boxes.

"Okay, here's what you're going to do," Cache said, a huge smile on his face. "And just listen all the way to the end."

Lance felt his hopes crash back to the ground with those words, but at least he could eat while Cache talked.

Sneak Peek! Last Chance Christmas - Chapter Two

Amber Haws woke on Saturday morning to the scent of hand sanitizer. The entire volunteer building smelled like it, as everyone had to clean their hands constantly. They used it when they entered the house to sign in. When they left. In every enclosure they went inside.

Honestly, the antiseptic scent turned her stomach.

As did the fact that she'd slept in the back room of the volunteer house in the first place. But she hadn't been able to face the twenty-minute drive back to her house. Alone. She was so tired of being alone.

Scratch that. She hadn't spent much time alone in the past couple of years. There were no shortage of men willing to ask her out, and Amber didn't have a problem saying yes. But she couldn't trust herself anymore.

She always picked the wrong guys to fall for. Dwayne had seemed so normal. So nice. So good.

"Fool," she muttered to herself.

She'd told her friends yesterday afternoon that she was done with dating, and Adele had told her to just give it some time. That she'd find the right man. If that was true, Amber couldn't see it.

She sat up with a sigh and ran both hands down her face. Exhaustion pulled through her, and she wanted a hot shower and a fresh doughnut. A dozen of them. In fact, all she wanted to eat today was doughnuts.

Normally, she didn't work weekends, but she'd putter around up at the ranch today, only so she wouldn't have to face her friends down in town and tell them about Dwayne. Detailing it for the women here at the ranch had been bad enough.

Regret lanced through her. She shouldn't have said anything to Scarlett. But she hadn't been able to work either, and she'd needed someone to help her check-out all the afternoon and evening volunteers. After all, she couldn't do it with tears streaming down her face and inexplicable anger rushing through her every time she saw a cowboy hat come through the door.

Or get in her car.

Double humiliation choked her at how she'd treated Lance Longcomb yesterday. He'd always been nothing but kind and thoughtful with her, and she wondered why he'd never asked her out.

They'd flirted shamelessly six months ago, but he'd never asked. Never said anything. She wasn't sure why. She thought she'd given him plenty of hints that she was interested in him.

Her phone buzzed, and she checked it to find Scarlett had texted. *Someone brought you breakfast this morning. Are you at the volunteer house already?*

Amber didn't want to tell her that she hadn't left. So she simply typed out, *Yep.*

She knew who breakfast was from—Scarlett herself. Well, probably Adele, though she only had a month left of her pregnancy and shouldn't be on her feet at all. But she was exceptionally skilled in the kitchen, and Amber's mouth watered just thinking about the stuffed French toast the woman made.

Amber hoped it was that. With bacon. A lot of bacon. *Candied* bacon.

And since she'd known Adele for a while now, Amber felt certain the woman would know about Amber's obsession with bacon.

You want me to bring it to you? Or do you want to come to the homestead?

Amber didn't want to re-hash everything. So she called Scarlett and said, "I'll come get it, but I don't want to stay."

"Lance is here. I can send him," Scarlett said.

Amber's heart skipped a beat. "Okay," she said. Then she could at least apologize to him for her behavior yesterday.

"Great," Scarlett said. "He's on his way."

Amber said, "Thanks," and hung up. If she was going to face the handsome cowboy and squeeze the words, "I'm sorry," from her throat, she needed to clean up first. She hobbled into the bathroom and turned on the water. She washed her face and slicked her damp hands through her hair, trying to tame the thick curls into something manageable.

She got them all gathered into a bushy ponytail and looked at her makeup-less face. It would have to do. As would yesterday's clothes. In fact, everything about Amber's life felt like yesterday's.

Used up. Old. Crinkled. Rusty. Dry.

Tears gathered behind her eyes again, but she sucked them back. She would not cry today.

She faced herself in the mirror, her eyes darker than she remembered. "Help me, Lord," she said. "It wasn't Lance's fault Dwayne was a jerk." She took a deep breath, feeling stronger than she had since the break-up phone call yesterday.

Her memory for a couple of hours there wasn't great, but she knew she'd almost run over Lance, and then she'd left him standing in the pouring rain.

As she left the bathroom, the front door of the volunteer house opened, and she came face-to-face with the gorgeous cowboy. Her breath caught in her lungs, as it always had when it came to Lance.

He carried a box of doughnuts, and surprise touched

her heart.

"Good morning, Amber," he said, finally coming all the way inside and letting the door close behind him.

"Morning," she croaked. Clearing her throat, she added, "I'm sorry about yesterday."

He waved one hand like what she'd done was no big deal. He was easy-going and laid-back, and she really liked that about him. "It was a rough day for you. I understand." He flashed a smile, the movement in his mouth quick and strong. "I also happen to know you love doughnuts."

He moved over to the counter where the volunteers usually checked in and set the box down. For some reason, Amber couldn't move as she watched him open the box. "Come see."

Their eyes met, and that electric charge that had always existed between them flowed as a live current. It propelled her across the space between them to peer down into the box. An array of chocolate and maple bars sat inside, and she couldn't help giggling.

As the tears came, she spun and grabbed onto Lance. "Thank you," she whispered into his shoulder, thrilled when his arms came around her too, holding her tight, tight against him.

"Listen, Amber." He coughed slightly and continued with, "I know it's not a great time and all that. But I've liked you for a long time, and I'd love to change your mind about cowboys."

Shock and fear made her pull away from him. "Lance—"

"Not right now," he said quickly, his bright blue eyes devouring her. "But I've always waited too long, and then some other guy asks you out. Some idiot like Dwayne." He leaned closer while Amber's mind spun.

I've liked you for a long time.

"So I just wanted you to know. I'm not Dwayne. That guy wasn't even a real cowboy." He took a step back and tipped his hat. "Enjoy your doughnuts." He fell back again, and Amber suddenly didn't want him to leave.

"Stay," she blurted. "I certainly can't eat all of these by myself."

"Yeah?" Lance asked, looking up from under the brim of his hat in the most adorable way.

"Yeah." She smiled and took out a chocolate bar. "Besides, I know you bought these for you anyway. I like the peanut butter ones more than chocolate."

"Oh, sweetheart," he said with a chuckle. "You think I don't know that?" He turned, opened the door, and stuck his hand out. Someone put something in it, and he turned back to her holding another box of doughnuts. He lifted the lid and tilted it toward her, and it only had peanut butter bars in it.

Amber blinked at it, warmth seeping through her, barely covering the surprise and the panic. She couldn't get involved with another man right now.

Could she?

Laughter filled her mouth, and she let it out. Lance laughed with her, and someone out on the porch of the volunteer house handed him a gallon of chocolate milk and a stack of cups, and then he locked the door behind him.

As they sat down behind the desk together to eat, Amber couldn't help looking at him again. He wasn't just a man.

He was the best-looking man she'd ever laid eyes on. The kindest.

And he liked her.

Had for a long time.

So maybe she couldn't get involved with another man right now, but she could certainly start dating a cowboy.

BY LUNCHTIME, Amber walked through her front door without feeling like the weight of the world rested on her shoulders. She'd had a great couple of hours with Lance that morning, and then he'd left with the words, "Whenever you're ready, Amber," and another adorable duck of his cowboy hat.

A cat yowled, and instant regret hit Amber again. "Cyclops," she said, dropping her purse a step inside the front door. "I'm so sorry." She got busy getting out more cat food, though the feline still had a bit of kibble in her bowl.

She was blind in one eye and declawed, but Cyclops still put off plenty of attitude as she waited for Amber to get the cans of wet cat food open. She paced, the cat equivalent of foot-tapping, and Amber kept apologizing until she put the food in front of the feline.

Cyclops dug into the food, and Amber went back to her purse to get her phone as it started ringing. JJ's name sat on the screen, and Amber swiped on the call. "Heya, sis."

A squeal filled the line, and Amber held the phone away from her ear. She giggled until her sister quieted, and then JJ said, "I just got engaged!"

Amber's heart dropped to the floor and rebounded back to its rightful spot in her chest. "Congratulations," she said, her voice hardly sounding like her own. In two weeks, Amber would turn forty, and that would make JJ six years younger than her.

Of course she had her whole life figured out already. Amber hated the poisonous thoughts in her head, but she didn't know what to do about them.

"Tell me how it happened," she said, hoping she could play the role of a supportive older sister for the next hour. She did wish happiness for her sister. Of course she did.

Cyclops finished eating long before JJ stopped talking, and the cat had apparently forgiven Amber, because she jumped into her lap and sat down.

"And I said yes." JJ sighed blissfully.

"That's so great," Amber said. "I'm happy for you, JJ."

"And you have to come shopping with me," her sister said.

"Of course," Amber said, letting some of the engagement excitement bleed into her. "Of course I will." She made plans with her sister for the following weekend, and when she hung up, she decided there was nothing better to do with her Saturday afternoon than take a nap.

Then she wouldn't have to try to make sense of her feelings. Wouldn't have to try to figure out why she couldn't find someone who wanted to commit to her the way JJ had. The way so many people around her had.

She closed her eyes, and the beautiful sight of Lance's face filled her mind. He'd said he'd be ready when she was, but Amber wondered if she should give herself some time before jumping right back into another relationship.

But that didn't mean she couldn't think of him every time she ate a doughnut.

Will Lance and Amber find a path that leads to each other? Or will this be their last cowboy Christmas together? **Find out in LAST CHANCE CHRISTMAS!**

Scan the QR code for a direct link to the paperback.

Last Chance Ranch Romance series

Journey to Last Chance Ranch and meet curvy, mature women looking for love later in life. Experience sisterhood, goat yoga, and a fake marriage against a stunning, inspirational ranch background—and some sexy cowboys too— from USA Today bestseller and Top 10 Kindle All-Star author Liz Isaacson!

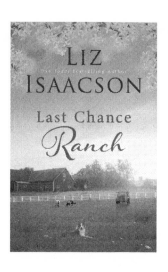

Last Chance Ranch (Book 1): A cowgirl down on her luck hires a man who's good with horses and under the hood of a car. Can Hudson fine tune Scarlett's heart as they work together? Or will things backfire and make everything worse at Last Chance Ranch?

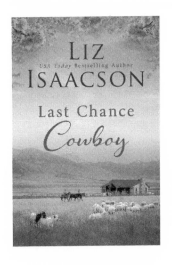

Last Chance Cowboy (Book 2): A billionaire cowboy without a home meets a woman who secretly makes food videos to pay her debts...Can Carson and Adele do more than fight in the kitchens at Last Chance Ranch?

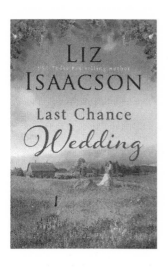

Last Chance Wedding (Book 3): A female carpenter needs a husband just for a few days... Can Jeri and Sawyer navigate the minefield of a pretend marriage before their feelings become real?

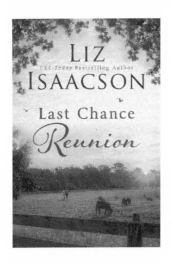

Last Chance Reunion (Book 4): An Army cowboy, the woman he dated years ago, and their last chance at Last Chance Ranch... Can Dave and Sissy put aside hurt feelings and make their second chance romance work?

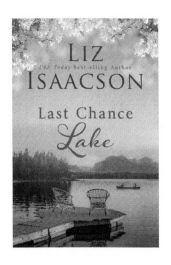

Last Chance Lake (Book 5): A former dairy farmer and the marketing director on the ranch have to work together to make the cow cuddling program a success. But can Karla let Cache into her life? Or will she keep all her secrets from him - and keep *him* a secret too?

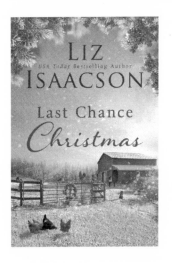

Last Chance Christmas (Book 6): She's tired of having her heart broken by cowboys. He waited too long to ask her out. Can Lance fix things quickly, or will Amber leave Last Chance Ranch before he can tell her how he feels?

About Liz

Liz Isaacson writes inspirational romance, usually set in Texas, or Montana, or anywhere else horses and cowboys exist. She lives in Utah, where she walks her dogs daily, watches a lot of Netflix, and eats a lot of peanut butter M&Ms while writing. Find her on her website at feelgood-fictionbooks.com.